KINDERGARTEN

Kindergarten

Peter Rushforth

Alfred A. Knopf   New York

1 9   8 0

This is a Borzoi Book
Published by Alfred A. Knopf, Inc.

Due to limitations of space, all acknowledgments
for permission to reprint previously published
material may be found on pages 191-2.
Library of Congress
Cataloging in Publication Data
Rushforth, Peter, [date]
Kindergarten.
I. Title.
PZ4.R95234Ki 1980   [PR6068.U76]
823'.9'14
ISBN 0-394-50917-X   79-3500
Manufactured in the United States of America
First American Edition

For the people
who gave me
their words

We only wanted to get away, only escape and arrive safely, nothing else.

Anne Frank. Wednesday, 8 July 1942

Whenever I close my eyes
I see them wander
There from this old farmhouse destroyed by the war
To another ruined house yonder.

High above them, in the clouded sky
I see others swarming, surging, many!
There they wander, braving icy blizzards
(Homes and aims they haven't any),

Searching for a land where peace reigns,
No more fire, no more thunder,
Nothing like the world they're leaving,
Mighty crowds too great to number.

From "Children's Crusade,"
Bertolt Brecht

KINDERGARTEN

B ESIDE a dark pathless forest there lived a poor woodcutter with his second wife and his two children, a little boy and a little girl. The boy was called Hansel and the girl Gretel. They had very little to eat, and when a great famine came to the country, the father found it impossible to find them any food at all. One night when the children were in bed, he lay thinking of what he could do for them all. Overcome with fear, he groaned, and said to his wife, "What can we do? How can we feed our poor children, when we can't even feed ourselves?"

"I know exactly what we can do, husband," answered the stepmother. "Tomorrow morning, very early, we will take the children into the midst of the forest, where it is darkest, light a fire for them, give them each one last piece of bread, and then we will go off to work, and leave them there, and never return. They will not be able to find their way home again, and we shall be free of them."

"No, my wife," said the father, horrified, "we cannot do that. I could not bear to leave my poor children alone in the forest. The wild animals will tear them to pieces."

"Fool!" said the woman. "If we do not do this, then all four of us will die of hunger. We must destroy them in order to live ourselves. Otherwise you might as well start making the coffins for us all now."

The man's heart grew heavy, and he would not agree with her. She did not leave him alone until he had agreed to her plan. He said to himself, "It is not right," and yet he agreed.

1

THE FACES in newspaper photographs and on television news reports had changed. The faces of terrified children, and of women holding up imploring hands, were no longer South-East Asian faces, but the faces of Europeans. The gun-fire, the burning buildings, the bomb explosions were in the streets of European cities once again. The unknown possibilities of death were all around.

IT WAS Christmas Eve, 1978.

The terrorists in the West Berlin school were making the captive children sing carols.

Children's voices came across the waste of snow in front of the school, the distant mass of the buildings showing no light from its windows. At first, Corrie thought they were singing "The Red Flag"—the tune was the same—but then he made out the words.

> "O Tannenbaum, o Tannenbaum, wie treu sind
>   deine Blätter!
> Du grünst nicht nur zur Sommerzeit,
> Nein, auch im Winter, wenn es schneit.
> O Tannenbaum, o Tannenbaum, wie treu sind
>   deine Blätter!

*O Tannenbaum, o Tannenbaum, du kannst mir
    sehr gefallen!
Wie oft hat nicht zur Weihnachtszeit
Ein Baum von dir mich hocherfreut!
O Tannenbaum . . ."*

The group of terrorists at the school were from the same terrorist organisation, Red Phoenix, as the people who had carried out the shootings at Leonardo da Vinci airport, the people who had killed his mother. He felt his stomach beginning to tighten. He had switched on the television to watch a cartoon version of "Hansel and Gretel," and the afternoon news report immediately preceded the children's programme.

Lilli, his grandmother, who had come through into their kitchen from her house next door, walked into the living-room behind him, drawn in by the German words. He turned to face her.

"What is that song?"

" 'Der Tannenbaum.' The fir-tree," she answered quietly. The words had awoken memories for her.

He thought of the special television news programme for the deaf on Sunday evenings, a digest of the week's events, when subtitles appeared at the bottom of the screen as the newscaster spoke.

Lilli sat beside him, looking at the television.

"The song tells us the fir-tree is a symbol of faith. It is always green, in summer, and in winter also, when it is snowing. We learn from it hope and steadfastness." She pulled a face as she spoke the last word, and looked interrogatively at him.

He nodded. The word was right.

"The fir-tree is noble and alone. It comforts and strengthens us."

She spoke each word very carefully, her mouth sometimes working awkwardly, as though the words were small solid objects she balanced between her lips. Her whole mouth puckered, as if she were about to pronounce the letter "o," like a child's when it has sucked something sour. It was only in her speech that the stroke she had suffered eighteen months ago occasionally left its sign, though strangers would not have noticed this, believing that her hesitancies were those of someone to whom English was a foreign language.

Her fingers were pulling the front of her smock.

"It was one of the few Christmas songs allowed in the time of Hitler. It makes no mention of Christ."

He looked at her face. Physical pain always faded as time passed. The memory of humiliation and mockery never died. Each time the memory was revived, the feelings returned as intense as they had been at the time they were first experienced.

She held her hand in front of him, opening out her fingers, and smiled.

" 'Der Tannenbaum.' "

He picked up the slender green fir needles from her open palm, smelling their freshness—snow in dark forests —noticing, for the first time, other needles clinging to the front of her smock and down her skirt.

"O Tannenbaum, o Tannenbaum," he said, and began to pick other needles from Lilli's clothes, dropping them into his cupped left hand.

He had once been a little afraid of Lilli. She was tall, still much taller than he, who was small for his age. She looked rather fierce, and now—in her seventies—was dressed in a loose billowing smock with a tiny dark floral pattern, and a rust-coloured floor-length velvet skirt. Her hair, still dark, hung loosely about her face, not like an old woman's at all. She looked like a folk-singer with a rich clear voice who would sing sad songs about the deaths of maidens, the cruelty of love—all the songs collected by his grandfather before his death. It was only in the last year that he had really talked to her, as he had helped to give her lessons after her stroke. His hands moved gently against the velvet material. Stroke. That was what a stroke was. A gentle touch of affection. A gentle touch on the brain that could cripple.

It was nine months since the killings in Rome. That had been during the Easter holidays. Mum would have been carrying Easter presents for them all. She had promised to get them all something.

The face on the television screen was a face at a window, the face of a frightened child. Below the child's face, the now familiar image behind the newscaster on each day's news, were the words "School Siege: Day Seven." They were marking the end of the first week of the siege by an extended news programme, the most coverage the event had had since the day it had started. As the number of days of the siege rose, news about the school had come later and later in the reports, moved to the inside pages of newspapers, shorter and smaller as the days went by, compressed by the greater demands of more recent events: a bomb explosion in Tel Aviv, a shooting at a Middle Eastern embassy in Rome, a plane hijacked from Belgium. The same pictures appeared over and over again: the air liner on a lonely desert strip, viewed from a distance across bare sand; the hooded figure at the window with the sub-machine-gun. The subtitles appeared and disappeared at the bottom of the screen, as if the words spoken were in a foreign language talking of incomprehensible occurrences.

Now the television screen showed the face of a weeping woman being restrained by a policeman wearing a peaked cap. She tried to pull herself forward, and away from him, towards the encircled school, her eyes gazing upwards.

The newscaster began to talk about the political situation in West Germany. Behind him as he continued speaking, filling the whole background, one brightly coloured picture remained as an image of modern West Germany. A group of well-dressed people were sitting in a glass-enclosed street restaurant in a pedestrian precinct. Stainless steel held the glass in place. It was very new, very sharp and shiny, like everything in the picture, the expensive clean impersonality of the transit lounge of an international airport, where all the people there were only passing through. Behind the glass, wiped free of all finger-prints, the men and women ate elaborate ice-cream confections from narrow cone-shaped glasses, the laden spoons held before their open mouths. Their eyes had the shut, closed-in look of people who knew they were being photographed but were trying to look natural. They all had rings on their fingers, men and women, and they were all middle-aged. Dim figures, many of them, could be seen through the dark glass which closed off the inner rooms of the newly painted building, but the door which led through from the outside, on which all the seated figures had their backs turned, was closed.

I N S I D E his copy of *Grimm's Fairy Tales*, lying on the floor beside him on top of the notebook with the ruled staves—spidery with pencilled notes, crotchets and quavers, much corrected—was the hidden postcard he had found in the school music rooms. He had opened the door set into the wall, and gone into the room beyond.

The postcard had been posted in Berlin in June, 1939, to the man who had then been the headmaster of Southwold School, a predecessor of his father.

Dear Mr. High,

Thank you very much for your kind letter. I am so
gratefull that you will receive me and my big brother in
your school. We wait now for permits. I send you our
good wishes. Dear Sir, also our parents thank you very
much. Excuse, dear Mr. High, all this troubles. Please
pardon me about my stammerings, but my will is stronger
than the words I know. We will be diligent in our study
and becomingness, and prove ourselves worthy. We will
be good boys. I am happy about my violoncello. Highly
esteemed sir, I remain,

                              Yours respectfully,
                              Nickolaus Mittler

Other pictures were shown on the television, some in colour, some in black and white: police photographs of
young men and women, unsmiling, staring straight ahead;
photographs of bomb damage; coffins being interred; bodies lying in streets, their feet protruding beyond the edges
of the blankets; people showing identity papers to police-
men; film of riot police with batons; crowds running from
tear-gas; burning buildings. Film of that day's events at
the West Berlin school was repeated, and the children's
high voices came from out of the darkness and the unlit
building.

Lilli held out her hand to take the fir needles from him,
and then stood up.

"How is the German Christmas?" he asked her.

She had spent the past week preparing what she said
was going to be a "traditional German Christmas" for
them in her house, insisting on doing everything herself,
keeping it all secret. Christmas Eve, she had told them,
was the special, solemn time, when everything important
happened. Christmas Day was not a special day. The fir

needles were a part of her plans. He had seen the fir-tree being delivered two days earlier. *Der Tannenbaum.*

"Six o'clock. The German Christmas will be ready at six o'clock."

O N   T H E other side of the postcard was a sepia photograph. *Die Freilichtbühne, Berlin. (Open-air Theatre, Berlin.)*

The scene was an enormous open-air theatre built to the same design as the theatres of ancient Greece. Tier upon tier of curved seating rose in an immense semicircle away and upwards from the circle of the orchestra, the dancing place for the Chorus. In the centre of that circle would be the altar. From the back centre point where the photograph was taken, the rows of seating arched away to right and left, the farther rows smaller and closer together. In the distance, behind the central grassed circle, was the acting area, a raised stone platform running the whole width from side to side, with a wide central flight of steps. Behind this was a high stone wall with an entrance facing the centre of the steps. Above and beyond the blank stone was a dark fir wood, its closely packed trees tall and impenetrable, the inner darkness beginning only a few feet from the edge.

There was no human figure in the whole scene.

The thousands upon thousands of seats were empty, and the stage was deserted. It appeared as ruinous and abandoned as the ancient Greek theatres on which it was modelled, waiting for some call, some sacrifice, to fill all those seats with rapt and fascinated spectators, engrossed and involved in some great tragedy, to purge the emotions of pity and terror: Agamemnon sacrificing his daughter to help him win a battle, *The Trojan Women, The Bacchae.*

In such a drama, very few would speak. The leading

actor would play several parts, surrounded by mute actors, and by the identically clad Chorus who moved in total unison. All deaths would take place off-stage, the slaughter of men, women, and children reported by a Messenger who would tell of what he had seen. Such drama was an act of worship, a reminder of the transience of man's life, a clear recognition of man's powerlessness in the face of mutability.

There would be the sound of a flute at sunrise, and through the central door on the raised platform a figure larger than life-size, wearing a huge tragic mask, raised up on high-soled boots, would enter and stand at the top of the flight of steps leading down into the circle. He would raise his head and look up at the tier upon tier of white faces surrounding him, rising higher and higher into the sky, before speaking the opening words of the tragedy which was to follow.

T H E   B O Y who had written that postcard had the same surname as the two brothers in *Emil and the Detectives*, the boys Emil had met in Berlin. Corrie remembered the younger brother, who usually never said a word, and the moment when everyone looked at him in amazement because he spoke—"Fish is so good"—and he flushed deep red and hid behind his big brother.

T H E   F I G U R E S in the restaurant reappeared. They all wore heavy coats, as if it were a cold country.

Lilli continued looking at the television for a while, and then went towards the kitchen, her hand cupped around the gathered fir needles.

" 'Hansel and Gretel'?" he asked. He had told her that

the cartoon was going to be on television, thinking it would interest her.

Lilli gave the suggestion her consideration, looking towards him.

She always looked with great intensity at whoever she was talking to, concentrating very seriously. He had seen her sitting and talking to Matthias, side by side, both un- aware of their surroundings, looking very hard at each other, like two statesmen working together to solve an almost insurmountable world problem. Her eyes were a very bright blue, not faded, as you would expect in an old person: all the colours about her were rich and deep.

Slowly she shook her head.

"No. I think not." She smiled, a little sadly. "No Han- sel. No Gretel." She spoke quietly. He turned to look at her face more closely, to recognise by her expression the quality of the emotion he had heard in her voice, but she had gone into the kitchen.

Her voice came back to him, louder. "The German Christmas will be ready at six o'clock."

"The English cup of tea will be ready shortly."

The news report ended, and the faces behind the flaw- less glass faded.

THE CARTOON which followed was not the story of "Hansel and Gretel" he knew, the little boy and girl in the painting on his bedroom wall, the story he was trying to put into music.

The first third of the story, a section he remembered vividly from when he was young (at his grandparents' house in Dorset, on holiday, Lilli's voice in his bedroom, the sound of the sea in the background), Hansel and Gretel's realisation that their father and stepmother were taking them into the forest to be torn to pieces by wild animals, was completely omitted. The old woman in the gingerbread house was made a grotesque and hideous fiend, not an apparently normal old woman, helpful and kindly, the sort of person one could meet at any time; and it was not made clear that Hansel and Gretel were going to be cooked and eaten by the old woman.

Some things were too frightening for children to know about, and who would wish to frighten children?

He switched off the television, and went into the kitchen. Lilli had gone through into her own house.

The style of the cartoon had borne little relation to the style of Lilli's illustrations for the story: the colours were garish, and the outlines crudely simplified. The precise detail and subtle colouring for which a Lilli Danielsohn water-colour was famous were entirely missing.

THE LITTLE boy and the girl, who was even younger, stood hand in hand at the edge of an immense dark forest, towering high above them, dressed in the fashion of the 1930s, the little girl with an elaborately woven shawl around her shoulders. They filled most of the picture, standing in the centre of the scene. The girl was looking in front of her, into the forest, and seemed frightened. The boy was looking over his shoulder, back the way he had come, looking straight into the face of anyone looking at the picture. The details were as intensely observed as in a Victorian genre painting, and the boy's open, unguarded face could be studied in the detailed way that one could only give to a face in a painting or a photograph, or the face of someone who was loved, and who returned that love. He looked as though he were trying to memorise what was behind him. A few crumbs of bread were lying on the ground just behind him. On the outer side of the two children were the shadowy figures of adults, enclosing them, grasping their arms, and leading them away.

CORRIE was Lilli Danielsohn's grandson, the grandson of somebody famous, somebody who had been forgotten and was being remembered again.

There had been a revival of interest in Lilli's work over the past year. There was an illustrated article in one of the Sunday newspaper colour magazines. A large-format colour paperback, *The Paintings of Lilli Danielsohn*, one of a series of art books, had been published some months earlier, and there were new editions of several of her books. Next year, another firm was producing Lilli Danielsohn greeting cards and posters, and there would be a Lilli Danielsohn calendar.

It was part of a fashion at this time, a nostalgic return to a rural past. In clothes, interior design, food, perfection seemed to be a re-creation of an idealised country cottage: tiny floral designs, simple colours, uncluttered interiors. There was a retreat from the present into the childhoods of another age, the illustrations from Victorian and Edwardian children's books.

Safe inside the ordered silence, people seemed to believe that the world beyond the window-panes would be sun-filled cornfields, empty of all but birdsong.

2

"FITCHER'S BIRD" was the first story from the
Brothers Grimm to be illustrated by Lilli Danielsohn. The
book was published in Berlin in 1929, the same year as
Emil and the Detectives.

O NCE there was a magician who could assume the
appearance of an ordinary poor man. In this form he
begged from door to door, and took away pretty girls. No
one knew where he took them, or what happened to them.
They were never seen again.

One day he knocked on the door of a man who had
three pretty young daughters. He looked exactly like a
poor old beggar, with a basket on his back, as if to carry
away any food or other gifts given to him. He begged for
just a tiny bite of food, and the eldest daughter, moved for
pity, came out to give him a piece of bread. He touched
her once, gently, and she was compelled to climb into his
basket. At once he sped away like the wind, leaving no
tracks, and took her into the heart of a dark pathless
forest, where his house was hidden.

It was a lovely house, and he surrounded her with
everything she desired. He said, "You will be happy with
me for the rest of your days, my love, for I have given you
everything you can ever wish for."

Seven days later he said to her, "I must go on a journey,

and leave you by yourself for a few days. Here are all the keys of the house. You may go anywhere in the house, and look at everything there is, but you must not go into one room, the room which is opened by this little key. If you go into this room, you will die, my love."

He also gave her a white egg, and said, "You must also protect this egg very carefully for me. You must carry it around with you at all times, for grave misfortune would result if you were to lose it."

He gave her the keys and the egg, and she promised to follow his instructions exactly. She watched him leave, and then began to explore the house, from room to room, from the cellars to the attic, looking closely at everything. The house was rich with silver and gold, and as she walked through the gleaming quiet rooms she thought that she had never seen such beauty.

Finally, she came to the forbidden door of the room she must not enter. She thought she would just walk past it, but she began to wonder what was behind that door. It was a door like any other door. She examined the little key carefully. It was a key like any other key. She put the key in the keyhole, turned it only a little, and the door was open.

What did she see inside that room?

An enormous bloody bowl stood in the middle of the room, piled with the dead bodies of human beings, hacked to pieces. Beside the bowl was a wooden chopping-block, and an axe which gleamed as brightly as the gold had done. She was so terrified that she let the egg fall from her hand into the blood-filled bowl. She quickly pulled it out, and tried to wipe the blood off with the corner of her dress, but the blood would not be removed. All day she washed and scrubbed, but the blood remained on the egg.

After seven days, the magician returned from his journey, and the first thing he did was to ask for the keys and the egg. She gave them to him, but she was trembling, and there were tears in her eyes. He saw immediately, by the bloodstains, that she had been in the forbidden room.

"You have been into the forbidden room against my will," he said quietly. "Now you shall go back into it against your own will. Your life is over." Calmly, he threw her to the floor, dragged her by her long hair, cut her head off on the wooden chopping-block, and hacked her body to pieces, so that her blood ran along the ground. Then he threw the pieces of her body into the bowl with all the others.

"Now I will go for the second daughter," said the magician, and again he went to the house in the form of a poor old beggar, and begged for just a tiny bite of food. The second daughter, moved for pity, came out to give him a piece of bread, and he caught her as he had caught the first, by touching her once, gently, and then carrying her away.

The same thing happened to her as had happened to her sister.

She was left with the keys and the egg, and opened the door of the forbidden room. She paid for it with her life when the magician returned.

The magician then went and brought the third daughter.

Seven days later he said to her, "I must go on a journey and leave you by yourself for a few days." He gave her the keys and the egg, and gave her the same instructions as he had given her two sisters.

The third daughter was thoughtful and intelligent. When the magician had gone, she hid the egg away very carefully, and then began to explore the house. Finally, she opened the door of the forbidden room.

What did she see inside that room?

Both her beloved sisters lay heaped there in the bloody bowl, murdered, and hacked to pieces. Weeping, she began to gather the pieces of their bodies together, and lay them out in order on the floor: the head, the body, the arms, and the legs. When all the pieces were lying together, they began to move, and the bodies were made whole again. The two sisters opened their eyes, and were alive once more. Then all three kissed and embraced each other very lovingly.

After seven days, the magician returned from his journey, and the first thing he did was to ask for the keys and the egg. There was no trace of any bloodstains on the egg, and he said, "You have passed my test. You shall be my bride."

He no longer had any power over her, and had to do whatever she told him.

"I shall be your bride," she said, "but you must first take a gift of gold to my father and mother, and carry it yourself upon your back in your basket. I will remain here, and prepare our wedding-feast."

She ran to her sisters, whom she had hidden away in a little secret chamber, and said, "The time has come when you can be saved. The magician himself will carry you home again, but as soon as you are home, send help to save me."

She hid both her sisters in the basket, and covered them over with gold, so that they were quite hidden. She then called for the magician, and said to him, "Here is the gold you are to take to my father and mother. Carry the basket to them. I shall be looking after you through my little window, and I shall see if you stop on the way to sit and rest."

The magician pulled the basket on to his back, and began to walk away with it through the forest, though it weighed him down so heavily that the sweat poured from him. After a time, he was so tired that he sat down, and wished to rest, but as soon as he did this, one of the sisters in the basket cried out, "I am looking through my little window, and I can see that you have stopped. You must go on again at once."

He thought it was his bride who was talking to him, got to his feet, and began to walk on.

He had walked a little further, when he felt tired again, and sat down, but the other sister immediately cried out, "I am looking through my little window, and I can see that you have stopped. You must go on again at once."

Every time he paused, or tried to sit down, the sisters cried this out, and he was compelled to move onwards. Finally, groaning and breathless, he arrived at the parents' house, with the gold, and the two sisters.

In the house in the forest, the magician's bride prepared the wedding-feast, and sent invitations to all the magician's friends.

Then she took a skull with its grinning teeth, put rich jewellery around it, flowers in its eye-sockets, and decked it with a garland, and carried it upstairs to her little window, so that it looked as if it were looking out. Then she cut open the feather-bed, covered herself in honey, and rolled herself in the feathers until she looked like a strange and wonderful bird, and could not be recognised.

As she walked away from the house and through the forest, she met the magician's friends on their way to the wedding-feast. They asked her:

> "Fitcher's bird, how did you come to be here?"
> "I have come from Fitcher's house, quite near."
> "Where is the young bride, and what is she doing?"
> "From cellar to attic all's sparkling and new,
> And from her little window she's looking at you."

Further along in the forest she met the magician, who was coming slowly back from her parents' house. He asked her the same questions as the others:

"Fitcher's bird, how did you come to be here?"
"I have come from Fitcher's house, quite near."
"Where is the young bride, and what is she doing?"
"From cellar to attic all's sparkling and new,
* And from her little window she's looking at you."*

The magician looked up, and saw the disguised skull in the window. He thought it was his bride, and called up to her. Then he and all his friends went into the house for the wedding-feast.

At this moment, the brothers and all the relatives of the bride arrived, sent to save her by her sisters. They locked all the doors of the house, and closed all the shutters, so that no one could escape, and set fire to it.

The magician, and all his friends, perished in the flames.

3

LILLI DANIELSOHN'S illustration for "Fitcher's Bird" was a water-colour, a double-page spread of a quiet interior flooded with warm light, a meticulous representation of a middle-class German bedroom in the late 1920s. On the extreme right of the picture, a beautiful dark-haired girl, the second sister, was beginning to open a door set into the bedroom wall. The curtains over the window were about to billow outwards into the room as the door opened. Plants on the window-ledge, a carved table, an oil-lamp, the individual threads in a woven bed-cover.

Beyond the bedroom door, unseen and unrecorded, was the mutilated body of her murdered sister. No blood seeped beneath the door into the image of domestic peace. In her left hand the girl held the fragile egg, which, when stained with blood, would mean that her life was over. Her face, in intense close-up, the eyes very large, did not look towards the forbidden room, but gazed out of the picture, towards the onlooker. She was very young.

AFTER Corrie had poured the boiling water into the teapot, he sat down to wait for a while before pouring out the tea.

The Kate Greenaway playing-cards Mum had fixed on the fridge door were still there. The six of diamonds had a picture of three little boys at the entrance to a churchyard.

We're all jolly boys, and we're coming with a noise. Mum.

He stared at the painted enamel eggs in the egg-cups on the pine dresser as he poured milk, and then tea, into Lilli's teacup, and poured out some orange-juice for Matthias. The nearest one to him was of two boys in sailor suits carrying a model yacht.

He took the cup and the orange-juice through into the sun lounge. The sun lounge ran the full length of the back of their house and Lilli's, and their kitchen and living-room both opened into it. He liked to hear the rain rattling against the glass roof. His parents had always referred to it as the sun lounge—ludicrous though that term was on a day like this one—perhaps thinking that the word "conservatory" had grandiose overtones, appropriate though it might be in an Edwardian house. Jo, his eleven-year-old younger brother, was more accurate when he called it the grot-hole. The floor was littered with Matthias's toys.

He pushed his way through carefully, bricks and model cars rattling across the tiles. He noticed a model soldier stuck in the soil of a plant pot near Baskerville's basket and wondered how it had got there. They had never been allowed toy guns, or any toys connected with war or war-games.

He peered through the glass, masking his eyes against the reflected light. He saw a torch approaching through the gravestones in the burial-ground, and the pointed hood of Jo's anorak as he skipped exaggeratedly along the path.

The connecting door between the two houses was in the sun lounge, and he walked through into Lilli's house. The floor of her sun lounge was equally cluttered.

Matthias, his three-year-old youngest brother, was there, kneeling on a chair up against the table near Lilli's hand-loom, leaning over a painting with immense concentration. His nose was dull green with dried paint. He was three years old, three feet high, and weighed three stone, a pleasing symmetry which Jo regarded as a strong argument against metrication.

The smell of cooking came through the open door from the kitchen.

"How's Horrible Horace?" Corrie asked, handing him the orange-juice. It was in a covered tumbler, with a little raised rim to drink from. He liked the special little things made for small children.

Matthias fell back into his chair, and surveyed the overall effect of his painting, like an artist checking his perspective, and then, very seriously, as though he were a French general bestowing an honour, he kissed Corrie on the cheek to thank him for the orange-juice. He was very lavish with his kisses with people he knew well.

"I'm not Horrible Horace!" he said.

"Murderous Matty? What have you done with my grandmother?"

"Making a German Christmas! I'm going to stay up late tonight!"

Matthias's voice always became very high and shrill when he was excited or amused.

"I bet you've eaten her. I can see a bit of her shoe in your teeth."

"What big teeth you've got!" Matthias shouted, adding, a moment later, "I'm not hungry."

Corrie walked round to look at Matthias's painting. There was a preponderance of green, applied in thick vertical strokes, and a large red blob at one side.

"What is it a picture of?" he asked.

"A havverglumpus," Matthias replied, with withering contempt. At least Corrie had looked at the picture the right way up this time.

He glanced around for somewhere safe to put Lilli's cup of tea, away from Matthias's paintbrushes. He noticed that her easel was out, at the edge of the sun lounge along from the loom, and wondered why Matthias wasn't using that. He eventually placed the cup on the bench in front of the loom.

This was the day when, in term-time, he and Jo came after school to have tea with Lilli. It was a tradition that had started some months ago, on a day free of orchestra practice and other school commitments, and they had carried it through into the holidays. Lilli would set out the table in the dining-room with flowers, a hand-woven cloth, and her best china, and they would spend an hour or so talking about the week at school, playing some of the new pieces they had learned on their instruments. He had grown to need those times with Lilli. Today they had suspended the custom, as Lilli was preparing the dining-room for her Christmas, but he had promised to bring her some tea.

He went further along the sun lounge, and then through the door into the living-room. Lilli's house still had two separate rooms downstairs, the dining-room at the front, facing out on to Dunwich Green, and the living-room at the back. In their house the two rooms had been knocked into one, and they had one long room running the full depth of the house, with an arch in the middle where there had once been a wall. Lilli's living-room was still waiting to be redecorated, bare and echoing, like a room in an empty house, the floor-boards uncarpeted, and the furniture under dust-covers.

He went through into the hall, passed the dining-room door, and picked up the evening paper from the floor beneath the letter-box. "CAROLS AT SIEGE SCHOOL." The subheadings in the report stood out: "POLITICS"; "TERRORISTS"; "HOSTAGES"; "DEMANDS." It seemed as good a summary as he had ever read of modern life in Western Europe.

He knocked on the dining-room door.

"Tea is served, modom."

"Thank you, my good man," Lilli said as she came out, using the phrase that Jo normally used when Corrie did something for him.

He offered her his arm, and they went through the kitchen into the sun lounge. Matthias sat sucking at the orange-juice as though he were plugged into the tumbler. He was always entirely self-absorbed when he was dealing with food or drink.

The sound of the rain on the sun-lounge roof was louder than it had been all afternoon. There was to be a carol service round the tree on Dunwich Green at eight-thirty. Jo was going to sing a solo.

"We need snow for tonight, not rain," he said to Lilli. "The more it snows—"

"Tiddely-pom!" Matthias said. He had finished his orange-juice.

"We can't have an Outdoor Hum for Snowy Weather when it's raining."

"And when we're indoors," Lilli added.

"I expect we'll get all the snow at Easter."

There had been snow on the ground when Mum had been buried.

He looked across at Lilli. She was sitting on the bench in front of the loom, holding her cup and saucer in one hand. There was a great quality of stillness about her. He had talked to her about most things, sometimes when Jo was not there, but he could not talk to her about what he had found in the school music rooms.

He leaned across Matthias, holding his little brother's painting up towards Lilli.

"What's this a picture of?"

"A havverglumpus, of course," she said, as if amazed that he hadn't known.

"Of *course!*" Matthias repeated, looking at Corrie with great scorn.

He climbed down from his chair, and went across to Lilli, then stood, legs apart and arms raised away from his sides, looking into the distance. Corrie stared at him, puzzled.

"Have you wet yourself?" he asked eventually, after Matthias had held the pose for some time.

"No! I'm being Rupert the Bear."

He was still standing like Rupert the Bear, and shrieking "Splishity-splash!" when Corrie went back into Tennyson's, their house, closing the connecting door between them. Tennyson's and Lilli's house were part of a terrace of Edwardian houses, each with a different white head above its arched doorway, gazing out across the Green.

Corrie's other little brother was in the kitchen, pouring out two mugs of tea. He was wearing his shiny green anorak with the hood up, dripping slightly, and green wellingtons. Wet footprints led through from the sun lounge, in which Baskerville, their elderly golden Labrador, was a wet panting heap.

Jo pushed a mug of tea across to him.

"How now, boy!" Corrie said.

"I am like you, they say."

"Why, there's some comfort."

Corrie and Jo regularly addressed each other through quotations, belabouring each other with their erudition. Jo was quite capable of keeping up with his older brother. Corrie had written the music for the school production of *The Winter's Tale*, performed a fortnight before the end of term, and they were still quoting that to each other. Jo had played the little boy Mamillius, and in the final scene of the play—off-stage, unseen, dead sixteen years—he had sung a song written by Corrie, " 'Tis time, descend, be stone no more," the music heard as Hermione, Mamilli-us's mother, stepped back into life to be reunited with her husband, Leontes. He had a beautiful singing voice.

"How's Lilli?" he asked.

"All prepared. Six o'clock."

He looked at the pointed hood, and Jo's sharp-featured face.

"You look just like a garden gnome dressed like that," he said.

"That's right," Jo answered, swinging his legs round. "I'm the National Elf."

He kicked his wellingtons off, hung his anorak on one of the hooks beside the door in the sun lounge, and began to unwind his long scarf round and round his head.

"The Ideal Gnome!"

He reached up for a biscuit from the tin with the repro-duction Victorian design for Colman's mustard, and then began to *entrechat* about the kitchen, jumping up and down and trying to stand on tip-toe, making extravagant sweeping arm movements, pirouetting through into the living-room. The paintings from school pinned on the family notice-board in the kitchen flapped as he went past.

"Curse this truss," he said eventually, and sat down, switching on the television.

He picked up the atlas that Corrie had been resting his music notebook on, and took out the pieces of the cut-up "Fitcher's Bird" illustration, sliding them into place. In an early lesson with Lilli, months ago, he had slit the repro-duction from one of his copies of the paperback, and cut it up into thirty pieces to make a simple jigsaw for her to put back together again.

" 'The heart of a dark pathless forest,' " he quoted as Corrie sat down beside him, carrying his mug of tea. They were both dressed in their best clothes, ready for the Ger-man Christmas, wanting to do the right thing for Lilli.

As the television picture appeared, a photograph of a blood-stained body filled the screen. The school siege was the main news again. The German terrorists had killed a woman who had tried to move up towards the school—the mother of one of the children. It was five-fifteen, and the special news bulletin for children was just beginning.

Jo leaned forward, and then jumped up to walk back through into the sun lounge. Corrie heard the clicking of Baskerville's nails as he slid around the tiles, and the occasional clatter as he ploughed through the heaped toys.

"We will execute all those who try to approach too near us," the Red Phoenix terrorists had announced. "We will make no concessions whatsoever."

He looked down at his tea. It was in a Peter Rabbit mug. Peter's mother was speaking to her children. He wondered whether Jo's dislike of Mr. McGregor in school was based upon a memory from early childhood.

Jo was obviously thinking about Mum again. He did his daft things, and made his quick comments as much as he ever did, but he did them automatically, his voice quite separate from the rest of him. And recently he had started having the nightmares again, the way he did for two months after Mum's death, when Dr. Disken had put him on some tablets to help him sleep. Last night Corrie had woken up at three o'clock and gone to the lavatory, and the light was on in Jo's room. He had gone into his room, but Jo was asleep, and he had left again after switching off the light—a little nursery night-light that Jo had had since he was three.

"Jo!" he called as the news came to an end. "Charlie Brown."

"Good grief!" came from the sun lounge in a chirpy small American boy's voice, but the cartoon had been started for some time before he came back into the living-room.

Small American children, serious and absorbed as any children in a Breughel painting, were discussing tactics in a baseball game they were about to play. Jo settled back, his head down at the base of the chesterfield, his feet, higher than his head, resting on top of a newly towelled and dishevelled Baskerville, who accepted his role as footstool with the weary resignation of a Snoopy. Jo laughed frequently, a high breathless chuckle, identical to the way Corrie laughed.

After the programme finished, there would be a five-minute programme for very young children, just before their bedtime, though he and Jo always watched it, usually claiming they were only watching it because Matthias was there. The current series was based on the Winnie-the-Pooh stories. Jo still had a battered Pooh that Mum had made for him. He called it his Linus's blanket. After this there would be the early evening news, and the picture of the murdered woman would fill the screen again.

Colour television had brought the colour of blood into the living-room. There was no dignity or privacy in death any more. Victims of road accidents or air disasters, murder or terrorism, had photographs of their destroyed bodies in newspapers or on television, to be looked at by strangers.

"We will execute all those who try to approach too near us. We will make no concessions whatsoever." The name of Rome airport had made Corrie see tall enigmatically smiling figures emerging from shadows, looking down over Mum's body lying on the blood-stained floor, pointing fingers, a ruinous Last Supper, notebooks filled with mirror writing, diagrams of unborn children in the womb. If they had had a television set nine months ago, perhaps they would have switched it on one evening to watch Piglet going in search of a Heffalump, and seen the body of their murdered mother lying awkwardly amidst broken glass on the marble floor of an airport lounge. She would have been wearing her green coat.

They had been sheltered in Southwold, within that quiet house in the little Suffolk town. The outside world had been far away, beyond the walls which surrounded the school grounds. The television was less than two months old. Things had happened far off, on the rim of a distant world, too far away ever to enter their quietude.

He picked up the two empty mugs and walked through into the kitchen.

Beside the sink was *The Wind in the Willows* calendar that Mum had bought last Christmas. It would be time to take it down soon. Christmas Day was circled, and the twenty-eighth of December, his birthday. He would be sixteen.

The December E. H. Shepard illustration was of the carol-singers outside Mole End. Mole was at the door, holding a candle, looking out at the group of tiny singing field-mice. It was a picture that seemed to him, like Lilli's illustrations, to carry an acute sense of sadness and melancholy behind it, a feeling of loss, and time passing. Perhaps it was just him, thinking of looking at the same illustration in the book when he was little, and Mum reading it to him. He sometimes felt that he would never feel as old again as he now felt, watching small children at play. He had a copy of *The Wind in the Willows* and other children's books near his bed, as carefully hidden as if they were pornography.

Above the illustration was the description of the carol-singers from the novel: *In the fore-court, lit by the dim rays of a horn lantern, some eight or ten little field-mice stood in a semi-circle, red worsted comforters round their throats, their fore-paws thrust deep into their pockets,*

*their feet jigging for warmth. With bright beady eyes they
glanced shyly at each other, sniggering a little, sniffing and
applying coat-sleeves a good deal.*

He ran the hot water into the mugs, wiping round the
inside with the cloth. He remembered a phrase from a
little further on in the novel, just before the words of the
carol: "shrill little voices." He could still hear the rain
beating against the glass roof of the sun lounge.

                                        London, N16
                                        30th March 1938

Dear Mr. High,

Miss Greif told me that you will accept my boy Walter
who has been at school in Berlin in your school at once at
the much reduced fee of £55. I do not know how to thank
you for your kindness. As I was well-off until only a short
time ago it was hard for me to ask you to moderate the
school fees. Miss Greif will have told you that I was a
musician in Germany, and as I am Jewish I have lost every
means of earning a livelihood there. I have been here in
England trying to begin a new existence. My wife and two
daughters are still in Germany waiting for the time when
I shall be able to support them here, and they can join me
and be safe. I hope this time comes soon. Mrs. Werth, Dr.
phil., was a lecturer and has now no more right to teach
in Germany.

My son will arrive in London this week. I have not
seen him for a year, and would like to have him with me
for two days, if you will allow me. Please do not send my
bill to my wife in Berlin, because of the special circumstances in Germany. She cannot write to you from Berlin
such as she wants to.

                              With great thankfulness,
                              Leon Werth

He heard the high urgent signature tune of the news beginning in the living-room, and then the television was switched off, and all the living-room lights.

Jo came into the kitchen, and walked through into the sun lounge.

"Hello," he said to Cyril, the umbrella plant on the desk. "It is I, Johann. Are you pleased to see me?"

He began to slide on the tiles, using his stockinged feet.

"Ready for the carol service, Jo? Warble, child; make passionate my sense of hearing."

Jo immediately assumed a coy expression, folded his hands in front of him, and began to sing in a very high-pitched voice.

> *"Once in royal David's city*
> *Stood a lowly cattle shed,*
> *Where a mother laid her baby*
> *In a manger for his bed:*
> *Mary was that mother mild,*
> *Jesus Christ her little child."*

"You're not singing that!"

Jo shook his head. "No. And not like that either."

He sat on the floor and began to put his shoes on.

"Do you know you're going mouldy, Corrie? I've tactfully refrained from mentioning it so far, knowing how sensitive you are about your appearance. One doesn't wish to cause embarrassment."

Corrie rubbed his hand across his face, and looked at the powdery green streaks from Matthias's poster paint.

"Just thought I'd mention it," Jo said.

"We were *always* singing that carol in junior school," Corrie said. " 'Away in a Manger,' 'We Three Kings,' 'While Shepherds Watched.' Do you remember hymn-singing in junior school?"

" 'Daisies Are Our Silver,' 'All Things Bright and Beautiful,' 'Little Drops of Water.' 'Please, miss, he had his eyes open during the prayer.' Mrs. Bradbury could never grasp the fact that if someone saw you with your eyes open, he must have had his eyes open as well."

"I remember you shoving your head up where the glove compartment used to be in that abandoned car, and pretending to be the radio."

"Hi there, all you listeners in wonderful radio-land."

"You never liked the Romans in Miss Pinion's history lessons, because they all went to the lavatory together."

"Filthy beasts!"

Jo was wandering restlessly about the sun lounge, touching at the window-frames.

"I wish I'd seen that nativity play with Matty."

"Just thinking about it makes me laugh."

During the previous week, Matthias had spoken of nothing but the nativity play which his play school had been taken to see at a local junior school, a special performance for an audience of mothers and grandparents. He had told them all about it. There was the Gold king, and the two other kings were called Frankenstein and Mirth. Frankenstein wouldn't kneel down, and Joseph's beard came off, and he dropped baby Jesus off the end of the stage. He bounced two feet into the air, and Guy Richens's grandmother laughed so much that she fell backwards off a bench, and everyone saw her knickers. Jo had enjoyed hearing that bit.

There was a pause.

Jo moved across towards Corrie, and sat down on the floor near Baskerville, scratching his head. He looked up at Corrie, his face serious.

"I wish Dad could be here with us for Christmas."

"He explained to us all about that, Jo, when he phoned. He explained all over again."

"*For Mum,*" Jo whispered, as though speaking an incantation.

"For Mum."

Four American children, members of a school group touring Europe, had also been amongst those killed at Rome airport. Their parents, together with others who had been bereaved, had formed the Sharon Schlechte Foundation, an organisation to aid victims of terrorism. Dad had flown to the United States a week ago, to help organise a fund-raising drive.

He had booked a phone call to them earlier that afternoon.

("Daddy!" Jo said, clutching the phone. It was a bad, congested line, like a dial being turned on an old-fashioned radio—the names of remote and unknown cities from outdated maps with pre-war boundaries—fragments of foreign phrases, the conversations of strangers, their father's voice half-drowned by the echoing voices calling out into the crowded air.

"Daddy!" Jo shouted out, trying to be heard across the gulf, all the voices in between.

"Everyone is so hospitable and kind, but I'm lonely here without you. I'm here because of Mum. What I'm trying to do is for Mum. If I could be with you, I would be. Christmas is a time for families.")

"Remember Lilli telling us that in Germany Christmas Eve is a time when the close family are alone together?" Jo spoke quietly, his head turned aside, as if he were whispering to Baskerville.

"Think of those children in Berlin."

IN THE silence that followed, all the lights suddenly went out. The kitchen clock began to chime six o'clock, and then, on the other side of the house, the school clock above the main building began to chime, the deep notes resounding across the Green. They were enclosed in a faintly gleaming glass box, watery shadows streaming down, as if they were below the surface of deep water, drawn down by the Nixie of the Mill-Pond.

On Lilli's side of the sun lounge there was a faint subdued glow, splintered by the frosted glass of the connecting door. As they watched, Jo still sitting on the floor, the glow grew in intensity, and swaying liquescent light came nearer. The door opened, and Lilli stood in the doorway, holding a candlestick in each hand. Illuminated by the soft, flickering light, her face intent, she was like a figure in a Gerrit van Honthorst nativity scene. Her hair was drawn back from her face, and she was wearing a simple floor-length dress.

Looking straight ahead of her, she began to make a formal little speech, her face impassive.

"A German Christmas is a very special time. Watch Night, *Weihnachten*, is associated with magical revelations. Mountains open and reveal their hoards of precious stones, church bells ring out from cities at the bottom of the sea, trees burst into blossom and fruit, the sun jumps thrice for joy, and the pure in heart can understand the language of animals."

She paused, and then raised her voice, calling out loudly, "Magical revelations!"

From an inner room in Lilli's house, a handbell began to ring, a high silvery sound.

"Come," Lilli said, standing aside from the door, smiling, beckoning them towards her, giving each of them a candlestick, placing her arms around their shoulders. "Come inside."

4

THEY followed Lilli through the darkened living-room, where Matthias was standing, immensely excited, ringing a little silver bell, and all of them moved slowly into the unlit hallway at the foot of the stairs, to wait outside the dining-room. The candles swayed in the cool currents of air, and, as they stood there, they could see the shape of the dining-room door outlined in a rippling light that shone through the gaps betwen the door and the frame from inside.

"This is the special room that no one has been allowed into," Lilli said. "Why did the bell ring?"

"Father Christmas has just gone!" Matthias shouted, very shrill, the bell ringing erratically as he jumped up and down.

"And what has he left for us in this room?"

The words were like a catechism.

"Christmas presents, and the tree, the tree!"

Matthias was in an ecstasy of expectancy.

"Open the door, Matty."

Lilli gave a small conspiratorial smile to Corrie and Jo as Matthias put his hand on the doorknob, hesitated rather nervously, looked round to see that they were still with him, and then pushed it hard so that it swung completely open.

There was a squeal from Matthias.

The whole room was green and silver, lit only by the

glow of scores of candles. The tree was the sole decoration, dominating the room, up to the height of the ceiling in the corner near the window, glittering with strands of silver hanging down from every branch, and for a moment —with the current of air gusting in as the door opened, and the heat and glow as they entered, the birthday-cake smell of burning candles—the whole tree, and the room, seemed to sway away and then back towards them as the shadows shifted. Candles covered the tree and rimmed the dining-table; and Lilli's glazed paintings, lining the walls, reflected back and multiplied the images of hundreds of candle flames, hovering in the air about them like bright fluttering wings. From the glass of every painting, from the polished wooden frames, from every reflective surface in the room—the face of the clock, the glasses and cutlery on the table, the metallic paper around the presents on the low tables in the bay of the window—light danced and pulsated, as if they were in a small and brilliantly lit church. Outside, in the cold and wet of the winter evening, the coloured bulbs on the bare branches of the horse-chestnut tree in the middle of Dunwich Green looked wan and distant, pale beyond the reflected glow in the dark glass of the window.

They were like some miniature religious procession as they moved into the room, advancing towards the altar for some service of memorial. As formally as she had made her little speech in the sun lounge, Lilli kissed each of them in turn as they stood around the table in the candlelight.

"This year we sit at the table and think of the members of our family who are not with us," she said quietly. Corrie glanced at Jo. They stood in silence for a moment with their heads bowed, and then sat down.

Meissen china plates—Corrie had seen them only once before—lined the centre of the table, filled with fruit, nuts and raisins, sweets, ribbons, tiny richly decorated spiced biscuits in ornate moulded shapes, hearts and diamonds, candied lemon and orange, iced stars with cherries, all beautifully arranged, and, as the centrepiece of the whole table, there was an elaborate and minutely detailed "Hansel and Gretel" gingerbread house, shaped just like the night-light Jo had in his bedroom. Steep-roofed, tiled with little twisted biscuits covered in Hundreds and Thousands, icing like snow dripping down from the overhanging eaves, its door partly open, it stood beneath the candles like the cottage beneath the trees in the heart of the forest, waiting for the approach of the abandoned children.

" 'Beside a dark pathless forest there lived a poor woodcutter with his second wife and his two children, a little boy and a little girl,' " Corrie said, looking at the gingerbread house.

" 'The boy was called Hansel, and the girl . . .' " Lilli paused, looking at Matthias.

"Gretel!" Matthias shouted. He looked across at Corrie. "I *do* feel hungry now. It's lovely, Lilli. It's lovely. I'm going to eat *everything!*"

He took his eating very seriously. You could take Baskerville's bowl away from him when he was eating, and he would only look very sad and miserable but make no objection. Matthias bashed people with his spoon.

Jo started to speak, Lilli smiled, and then everyone was talking, and the muted solemnity of the beginning—an Easter mood, a Good Friday mood—became animated and lively, and Lilli, after talking with them, went out of the room towards the kitchen, to bring in the first course of the Christmas meal.

AS THE meal continued, the unfamiliar weight of the silver cutlery in his hands, Corrie became convinced that Lilli, with her German Christmas, was not re-creating something she had herself once experienced, an expatriate, after many years, feeding the nostalgia for a ceremony in which she had once taken part. The speech in the sun lounge had not been her words: she had been quoting something she had read, and all he saw around him, carefully and beautifully contrived, was as novel to her as it was to them, possibly inaccurate, a creation from books and research, not from memory. Christmas was a feast she would never have kept when she was in Germany, because Christmas was not a Jewish festival.

He had a secret, sort of, about himself.

Like Nickolaus Mittler and his big brother, like Leon Werth and his family, he was Jewish, and he had not known it until two years ago. As Lilli was Jewish, then, by the rulings of Germany in the 1930s, he himself—Gentile and uncircumcised—was also Jewish, a *Mischling*, Second Degree, a child with one Jewish grandparent, descent through the female line being Jewish Law. It was something inside himself, something in his blood.

It had been Christmas two years ago when he had found out about Lilli Danielsohn. The name had been a strange one to him, an unfamiliar disguise in someone he had known all his life. To him, his grandmother had always been Lilli, and, sometimes, when he wrote to her to thank her for presents at Christmas or on his birthday, she was Mrs. Meeuwissen—his father's mother—when he addressed the envelope, someone with the same surname as himself. Her German accent was just the way she spoke.

Lilli, like the girl bound to silence in "The Six Swans," had never spoken a word about her past, her life in Germany, her family; her books and paintings had remained locked away, from herself, and from everyone else. Four years ago, Grandpa Michael had died, and Lilli had left the house where the two of them had lived in Dorset, and moved to London. In London, living alone, her husband dead, she had begun to look at the paintings again for the first time in forty years.

When she had been there for two years, they had gone from Southwold to see her. She had changed—become very quiet and introspective, not the seemingly stern and commanding woman he had always known—and the little London house had seemed bare, a place without memories, as if she had no past she could place around her; but on the evening of the first Sunday of their stay, when they were talking around the fire, he had found out about Lilli Danielsohn. The things she had not spoken about for all those years were said—a decision she had come to before they arrived. It was something she had wanted to talk about.

She had spoken of places and events from history books, enclosed within dates—(1933–1945)—like the life of someone famous who had died, or the duration of a war that had ended long ago. But these historical events, these dates, had been a part of her life. She had lived through them. She had been there. When she married Grandpa Meeuwissen in 1939, she had been a refugee from Germany: his parents had known this much, though he and Jo had not. When she had left the country in 1938, to arrive alone and unknown in England, she had been famous throughout Germany as an artist. Her first book, *Kinderstimmen*, a series of illustrations for German poems about childhood, had been published in Berlin by Ullstein in 1924, in the same week as *When We Were Very Young* was first published in London. Her work had met with increasing success in the late 1920s and early 1930s, until, in 1933, the Nazis had come to power. Copies of her books had been burned by the Nazis in Berlin in 1933, in Unter den Linden, between the Opera House and the University. The children's stories had gone up in flames, like Erich Kästner's books, with the works of Freud, Marx, Mann, Heine, and all the others, because she and her family were Jewish. She had been unable to publish any more of her work.

That evening, hesitant and shy, she had taken her paintings out of the drawer in the roll-top desk where she had kept them locked up all those years, unglazed, loose in cardboard folders, and shown them. His parents had never known that she had been an artist. Since she left Germany, she had not painted again.

He would never forget that evening, and his first sight of the paintings he now knew so well, all around him on the walls of the dining-room. She had given each of them one of her original water-colours for a Grimm's fairy-story as a Christmas present. His was the illustration for "Hansel and Gretel," the painting beside his bed that he studied each evening. It was the first of her paintings that he had seen, and he thought it very beautiful. It was the loveliest present he had ever been given.

She had embraced them all when they left to return to Southwold.

They visited her again in the summer, and she had seemed a lot older.

He saw her one evening, thinking she was unobserved, walking about the small garden like the personification of Sorrow in a morality play, bent over, walking up and down as the light began to fail. He was afraid to approach, shrinking away from her deep and private source of grief, her numbed face that looked as if it had been exposed to intense and prolonged cold. Seeing her like this, he thought of someone carrying and shielding a flickering candle in a wind-swept corridor. Thoughts in her head, like candles on a child's birthday cake, dipped and bent, but never flickered out into darkness. The small intense flames were always there. Her eyes had the blind unfocused stare of someone who had gazed too intently into

the candle flame, and who carried a dark shadow im-
pressed deep inside the eye.

Several months later, she had suffered her stroke, and
after some time in hospital, Dad had brought her from
London to live next door to them, with the connecting
door between the two houses, and the months of recovery
and teaching had started, and he had come to know someone new, a Lilli who was not the woman in the bare house
or the dark garden.

In novels, particularly in Victorian novels, the author invented a complete family history for his characters,
and, as the reader, one could know more about the his-
tories of these fictitious families than one knew about
one's own family history: this, Corrie supposed, was part
of the pleasure of fiction. It had struck him as slightly
wrong that the characters always seemed to possess an
awareness of every detail of their family history—unless a
startling discovery were a major part of the plot—feeling
themselves firmly placed in a structured and predictable
family tree. His life had been lived with blanks and ab-
sences, emptinesses that he had been too uninformed or
too reticent to explore.

Discovering his Jewishness—it couldn't be denied,
could it?—he felt as though he had opened some forbidden door, made some shocking discovery which over-
turned all the certainties in his life. He felt as though he
had suddenly discovered that he'd been adopted, and that
all his assumptions about his parentage, all his beliefs
about who he was, were completely false. He had no con-
crete dogma to hold on to, no self-protecting litany to
chant like the song of the bird in "The Juniper Tree." It
had sounded so odd when Lilli had spoken about "marry-

ing an Englishman"—Grandpa Michael—and "becoming
a Christian." He knew hardly anything about the Jewish
religion, had never even spoken with anyone about it.
Once, in the summer holidays, he had gone with Cato Levi,
his friend at school, to a demonstration outside the Soviet
Embassy against the treatment of a Jewish dissident, but
he had felt quite separate from all those angry young people, who seemed sure of who they were and what they
wanted. He had been a little bit frightened.

In Lilli's house in London, amongst her many books,
there was a copy of *The Children's Haggadah,* a book
published in 1937, which he had looked at, curious and
confused, in the days after that Sunday evening, to try and
learn something about the Jewish religion, feeling as
though he were reading about an invented religion in a
mythical land called Rousseau, a Middle Earth, a Narnia,
an Earthsea. The book read from back to front, and on
the back cover was a picture of a small child in a skull-cap
lying asleep in bed, clutching the book in his arms. Inside,
little pieces of card could be pulled from side to side to
make the pictures move: the baby Moses floated down the
Nile in his basket, the Egyptian army sank beneath the
sea. *On the evening before the eve of Passover, the father
of the family goes into every room of his house to see
whether all leavened food has been cleared away. It is
customary to place small pieces of bread in every room,
and the father collects them carefully by the light of a
candle. These are burned on the following morning soon
after breakfast.*

If he had discovered that he were a Roman Catholic,
and had not known it, he would have felt the same suffo-
cating approach of things of which he knew little: candles,
rosaries, rich vestments, and confessions of one's most
secret thoughts to an unknown man. But he had at least

been in a Catholic church. He had never been inside a synagogue. He had seen one once, from a car, and it had seemed an intensely enclosed and private place, a windowless façade, inward-looking, a place to which no strangers could ever be admitted.

THE LIGHTS began to dim, like a coal fire settling. Candles began to gutter and go out, one by one, as the meal came to an end. When the candles were all out, they would start to unwrap their presents, opening gifts in the evening, with the birth, not waiting until the following morning, after the child had been born. He looked around at the shifting luminescence of the many candles. Wasn't there a Jewish festival called the Feast of Lights? Was it a feast of rejoicing, or a mourning for the dead? All the candles, flickering across the glass of the water-colours, the figures indistinct in the blurred air, were like the memorial candles one lit in churches on the continent.

If there was any self-portrait in Lilli's illustrations showing her as he had seen her that Christmas two years ago, it was the illustration of the mother in "The Wilful Child," the shortest story she had ever illustrated, only a third of a page long. It was the final illustration in the last book she had published in Germany, at the very beginning of 1933.

The mother, a young woman in her early thirties, bent over the grave of her child, looking with great intentness at the child's arm, which stretched upwards out of the soil, refusing to be buried. In her hand the mother was holding a branch, with which she was attempting to strike at the arm, so that the child would withdraw its arm beneath the ground, and lie at peace. The expression on this mother's face he had seen on Lilli's. The curious ambiguous mixture of anguish and determination was the expression of a woman trying to will herself to creep up and smother a much-loved child who was dying painfully of a lingering illness.

THE MAIN frontage of Southwold School filled the south side of Dunwich Green, the southernmost of all the Greens in Southwold, and in Lilli's dining-room the sound of the school clock from the tower was clear and distinct as it struck seven o'clock. A short while later, the mechanical bells of the clock above the restaurant on the side of the Green opposite the school struck the hour, followed by the chiming of the music for the folk-song "Long A-Growing."

They moved away from the table to group around the fire. They sat in the dimming light, a cave of chiaroscuro, like Lilli's illustration for "Snow White," the little girl kneeling on the chair in the country cottage, reaching up towards the open window where a hand appeared, holding out half an apple to her. On the table nearest to Corrie was an oddly shaped parcel, labelled "To Baskerville, with love from Jo." He signed his name "jO," with a small "j," and a smiling face—two dots and a curve—inside a very large "O." There was a separate table for each person's presents.

Until the candles burned fully down, before the presents could be opened, they were to read, play music, and recite poems they had newly learned by heart. Lilli had asked if they would do this, a week before Christmas, after Dad had left to drive to Heathrow airport, the same day the terrorists had entered the Berlin school. Corrie and Jo were both used to performing, particularly music. Corrie had started an Elizabethan consort in school, the Elizabethan World Picture, and Dad, Mum, he, and Jo had regularly played together, for friends and relations, or by themselves, a family in a quiet room, absorbed in a piece of music together. Their instruments were ready, set out for them by Lilli. They had practised their pieces in the music rooms.

Lilli began by reading the story of the nativity from St. Luke's gospel, words of scripture—"swaddling clothes," "a multitude of the heavenly host"—that had been a part of the mind since early childhood, like some hymns, and certain poems and stories, as if they had always been there, a rhythm of sound that awakened memories of the time before the words had been understood.

When Lilli had finished reading, Jo stood up and began to sing, in his clear, pure voice, "In the bleak mid-winter," the carol he was going to sing in the service on the Green. Lilli was not going to come out into the rain and cold, though Sal was coming round later that night, and Matthias would not have been alone in the house. Sal and Lilli would watch from the dining-room window.

Everyone applauded when he had finished, and he bowed to each of them in turn.

"Thank you," he said. "Unexpected and gratifying, if a little lacking in Smack."

It was Corrie's turn now.

He brought over one of the dining-chairs, and sat down with his cello, spending a long time shifting his position until he was completely satisfied. Jo, standing beside him, looked at him for his signal.

Corrie took a deep breath. They were going to perform one of the songs he had written for "Hansel and Gretel." He had found the words in *Kinderstimmen*, the final poem in the book: "Auf meines Kindes Tod." It was by Joseph von Eichendorff, a nineteenth-century German writer. He had got Jo to learn it in the original German.

"This is especially for Lilli," he said. "You won't recognise the music, but I think you'll recognise the words."

He felt very nervous of playing this in front of other people, even though they were people who had often listened to music he had written, but Lilli had given him a part of herself in giving him her painting: he would now give her a part of himself in return, a piece of music he had written himself.

He nodded at Jo and, bent over the cello, began to play the long piece of wordless music before the song began. At the exact moment he moved into a higher key, Jo began to sing:

> *"Von fern die Uhren schlagen,*
> *Es ist schon tiefe Nacht,*
> *Die Lampe brennt so düster,*
> *Dein Bettlein ist gemacht.*
>
> *Die Winde nur noch gehen*
> *Wehklagend um das Haus.*
> *Wir sitzen einsam drinnen*
> *Und lauschen oft hinaus.*
>
> *Es ist, als müsstest leise*
> *Du klopfen an die Tür . . ."*

The illustration of the empty cradle was on the wall opposite them.

When he had finished playing, Corrie held his position for a moment, and then relaxed, leaning back and looking across at Lilli. She was gazing across at the painting, holding tightly on to Matthias as he sat on her knee, lying against her. She said nothing for some time, and then looked at him.

"You wrote that music, Corrie, didn't you?"

He nodded.

"I have never heard that poem as a song before, but your music made it into a beautiful one. Thank you."

After they had listened to some poetry, and Matthias had sung a song he had heard on the radio, the same line over and over again, Jo played a gavotte on his flute, composed for him by Corrie, as Matthias did one of his dances, jigging from foot to foot, and turning round and round. The last candle finally went out as Corrie was playing his cello. They listened in the darkness, in the firelight, until he had finished, and then the lights were put on and the presents opened.

C O R R I E had just finished drying the last plate when Jo, who had finished his share of the washing-up a short while before him, reappeared in the kitchen.

"Come and listen!" he whispered, signalling to Corrie like a very small boy expressing urgency in an old black-and-white film.

Corrie moved out into Lilli's hall, closing the kitchen door behind him, moving very quietly, caught by Jo's mood. He sat down on the bottom stair, beside Jo, his feet next to some of Matthias's scattered toys. There was a little woolly bear that he remembered Mum buying him in Bamburgh when he was seven. He picked it up and dangled it by one of its paws.

From upstairs they could hear Lilli telling Matthias the story of "The Wolf and the Seven Little Kids." Matthias had come down, washed and dressed for bed, when they were in the middle of doing the dishes, to kiss them both good night. Jo sat with his knees pulled up against his chest, and his head leaning on its side on top of them, listening very intently.

" 'The seven little kids cried, "You must show us your paws first before you can come in, so that we will know that you really are our dear kind mother." So the wolf put his flour-covered paws in through the window, and when the little kids saw that they were white, they believed that he really was their mother, and they opened the door. And in came the wolf! They were terrified, and . . .' "

Lilli sounded quite anxious. She always read stories well.

They listened a little longer.

"Corrie, do you remember when Mum used to read me that story?"

Jo's face was turned away from Corrie, and he could not see his expression.

"Yes, I do."

"That time when I had asthma really badly."

" 'In tears,' " Lilli was saying upstairs, " 'the mother goat called out the name of her youngest child, and a little voice said, "Mother, dear mother, I am hiding in the clock-case." ' "

Jo pushed at the bear that Corrie was holding by its front paws, until it rocked backwards and forwards.

"When we were in the dining-room, before we opened the presents . . ." Jo began. "When we were there, performing for Lilli, it reminded me of the Victorian Evening."

"Yes."

"That was the last time we saw Mum, and we didn't realise."

Jo's hair was tousled from where it had rubbed against his knees.

On the Sunday night before Mum had flown to Rome, they had put on a Victorian Evening for Lilli, who was still suffering the after-effects of her stroke. Dad had driven Mum to the airport early the following morning, when he and Jo were still in bed.

Then, unexpectedly, Jo smiled.

"I'll always remember that evening."

Jo had drawn a programme for Lilli in a variety of

elaborate Victorian type styles, and they furnished the window-bay of Lilli's dining-room like the corner of a Victorian drawing-room, carrying through the scrap-screen from their living-room, moving the chaise-longue round, and putting Jo's model theatre on a small tripod table and Cyril—deputising for an aspidistra—on a *jardinière* from the sun lounge. Wearing Victorian clothes, they performed for an hour, with Lilli as their only audience. They acted part of *Lady Audley's Secret*, with Jo, who rapidly assumed a woman's costume, a memorable Alicia. Mum was Lady Audley. They read the death of Little Nell; extracts from a handbook of Victorian etiquette; "Casabianca," "Lips That Touch Liquor Shall Never Touch Mine," among other poems—and sang several Victorian songs. The one Corrie remembered best was Mum and Jo singing "Won't You Buy My Pretty Flowers?"

Upstairs, Lilli was reaching the end of the story.

" '. . . the heavy stones made the wolf fall into the well, and he was drowned. When the seven little kids saw what had happened, they came running up to the well and shouted for joy, "The wicked wolf is dead! The wicked wolf is dead!" They danced around the well with their mother.' "

Jo pushed at the bear again, and it fell to the floor.

He was bending down to pick it up when the doorbell was rung, three times, in a signal they recognised.

"Sal."

Sal had been Mum's closest friend, and was a regular caller at both houses.

When Corrie opened the door, she staggered in, struggling with her umbrella and several parcels, as if she had been given a violent push in the back. She groaned, leaning back against the door, straining to close it.

"What a night!"

She dumped the parcels into Corrie's arms, and bent
down to kiss him on the cheek. He was still only five feet,
three and one-half inches tall.

"Happy Christmas, gorgeous."

She ran her hands through the tight curls of her newly
permed hair, shaking out the wetness, and brushed at the
front of her clothing. Then she peered closely at Corrie's
hair, assuming a scowl. She claimed to be deeply resentful
of Corrie's dark curly hair, a style she could only achieve
by visits to the hairdresser's.

"You're not really letting poor little Jo sing out on the
Green in this weather, are you, you rotten swine?"

"Did you call my name, belovèd?" asked Jo, standing
up and striking a dramatic pose.

"Can it be he?" Sal said, clutching her hands to her
heart as she turned to face him.

"My own!" he called. "I yearn to be with you! Clasp me
to your bosom! Madden me with desire!"

Jo dived into Sal's arms, and she hoisted him up into
the air, his feet dangling, and pressed him against her.

"My angel!"

It was a performance they went through regularly, once
in the middle of Norwich market-place when they had
seen Sal there. A stall-holder had offered Jo a cauliflower
to swap places with him.

"Can we tone down these scenes of unbridled passion?"
Corrie asked.

"Heavens, we're observed!" said Jo, his voice rather
muffled.

Lilli was coming down the stairs.

"I like that new pendant you've got round your neck,"
she said to Sal. It was the first time she had joined in one
of their silly sessions.

Sal started laughing, and dropped Jo.

"He's too heavy to wear for long," Sal said. "You've been feeding him up again."

"We've left you a few scraps," Corrie said. "Mind that lump in the carpet."

Sal stepped over Jo, and took Corrie's arm as they went through into the dining-room.

"DO YOU happen to have the time on you?" Corrie asked later, as they walked through Lilli's kitchen towards the sun lounge. He had been asking Jo the time every quarter of an hour or so since Jo had unwrapped his present. Corrie had given him a combined Christmas and birthday present, an expensive gift that he had been saving up for for some time: a Snoopy wrist-watch, with the dog's front legs as the hands of the watch. Clutching a tennis-racket in one hand, Snoopy lugubriously swung his arms round and round the dial.

Exaggeratedly, Jo pulled back the cuff of his shirt and moved the wrist with the watch on up towards his face, twisting his wrist from side to side so that the watch faced towards him, then away.

"The time by my brand-new Snoopy watch is eight-oh-seven precisely."

"I say, what a spiffing watch!"

Corrie and Jo often spoke in the slang of old-fashioned school stories, assuming a painfully genteel and high-pitched accent, parodying their fictional roles.

"Santa brought it for me. I can tell the time now!"

"How *super!*"

The lights were on again on their side of the sun lounge, and in the kitchen. Baskerville was lying in his basket beside the desk with an expression of utter abandonment and desolation on his face. He lumbered to his feet as they came in, looking guardedly pleased.

Jo waved the parcel he had brought through from Lil-li's, and began to circle around Baskerville.

"I've got a prezzy for you!"

Corrie heard them chasing each other about the sun lounge as he went through into the kitchen, and then into the living-room, leaving the light off. He looked out through the front window towards the tree in the centre of the Green. No one was there yet.

There were bangs and slitherings from the back of the house, and Baskerville barked a couple of times. Corrie sat in the dark for a short time, and then went back through into the sun lounge. Baskerville was stretched out on the floor, chewing an enormous bone.

"I got him so excited that he wet himself," Jo said, wiping at the tiles with a mop. "I've never had that effect on anyone before."

Baskerville, grasping the bone on its end between his two front paws, shifted his position slightly, and the bone fell forward and hit him sharply on the nose. He looked startled, and scrabbled backwards.

"Baskervilles don't like bones."

Jo put the mop and bucket back in the corner, and then walked towards Corrie. He raised his eyebrows, pulling the corners of his mouth down in an expression of inno-cence. He had an extraordinarily mobile face, his features always shifting. When he talked, every particle of him took part in the performance. He could make Corrie giggle very easily sometimes, by just looking at him.

"I have my theories about you and Sal," he said. "The whole thing became clear to me when you sneaked away into the dining-room together, leaving me lying on the floor."

"And I thought we were being so discreet."

"It's obvious. She's studying you to use in her next

novel. In the interests of research, writers are sometimes compelled to undergo some very unpleasant experiences."

"Do you think that my perversions . . ."

"Many and varied though they are . . ."

". . . are advanced enough to interest her?"

Sal was quite well known as a writer of novels for young people—"New Adults," they were called by the publisher—usually dealing frankly with complex emotional or sexual difficulties.

"You could work on them a bit," Jo said. "Show a bit of imagination." He looked at Baskerville. "Why not have a passionate affair with Baskerville? I don't think she's used that one yet."

Baskerville, looking vaguely troubled, edged away and eyed Corrie with deep suspicion.

"He doesn't look too keen on the idea."

"Poor old Baskerville. The dignified butt of vulgar jesting."

Jo began to stroke Baskerville's head, and then continued speaking. "She *is* good, though, isn't she?" he asked. "Her novels."

"*Stephen's Child* is."

"Not as good as *Small for His Age*."

"Just because it's about you."

"Judging by the title. Actually"—Jo's voice became excruciatingly cultured—"I warmed to the subtle nuances of the adverbial clauses . . ."

"Well-educated infant!"

". . . reminiscent, one feels, of the later period of Henry James."

"One does indeed. One also thrills to the shimmering evocativeness of the setting."

"And the daring audacity of the semicolons."

"And the enormous bosoms."

"And the enormous bosoms." Jo giggled. "If it did have those, it might explain why people are so *rude* about Sal's books."

"Never a week goes by without some headmaster having heart failure."

"This book . . . This book . . ."—Jo began to keel over in slow motion, an expression of apoplectic horror on his face—"contains scenes of . . . *masturbation!*"

"Whatever that might be."

"Whatever that might be."

Corrie looked at his watch. "The carol service will be starting soon."

Jo searched for his wellington boots under the table.

"I expect we'll be the only people there. When they tell you that you're singing a solo"—his voice became suddenly effete—"one does tend to imagine that one's not completely solo, and that there will be people there to listen to one."

"One does."

"I'm the vicar in the empty church."

"Verily."

Jo stood up and put the wellington boots on.

"I'm going to sing whether anyone's there or not."

He looked at the wooden weather-house on the dresser. Both figures, the man and the woman, were inside the house, their backs turned on the outside world.

"I know just how you feel," he said.

The telephone began to ring in the hall.

"I bet I know what that's about," Jo said, and went out.

He came back in a few minutes later, nodding his head. "Cancelled?"

"Cancelled. I'll just go and tell Lilli."

When he came back in, Jo pulled on his anorak and took down Dad's umbrella.

"I said I was going to sing whether anyone was there or not."

Corrie made a move towards the hallway, to go out to the Green from the front door, but Jo went through the sun lounge and opened the door into the garden at the back.

"Come on," he said to Corrie. "Quick, before Basker-ville makes a break for it."

Corrie had to bend down, sharing the umbrella with his brother, bumping into him, standing on his heels, until he took it from him and held it over both of them. Jo led him out on to the path which ran alongside the end of the garden, along the top of the low cliff above the beach. He turned left towards Gun Hill, and some time later, wet and breathless, they were walking into St. Edmund's church-yard.

He followed Jo, to stand in front of Mum's grave.

Jo took a torch out of his anorak pocket, and they looked at the writing on the gravestone.

There was a bunch of copper-coloured chrysanthemums on the grave, their petals separated and scattered about.

"They didn't last long in the rain," Jo said.

Then, just as he had done in Lilli's dining-room, he began to sing, naturally and unself-consciously, his head back, his hands thrust into his anorak pockets, his voice perfectly distinct above the sound of the rain on the um-brella.

> *"In the bleak mid-winter*
> *Frosty wind made moan;*
> *Earth stood hard as iron,*
> *Water like a stone;*
> *Snow had fallen, snow on snow,*
> *Snow on snow,*
> *In the bleak mid-winter,*
> *Long ago . . ."*

As Jo sang, Corrie felt again the mood he had entered looking at *The Wind in the Willows* calendar in the kitchen, and hearing the words of the nativity at Lilli's: the sense of time passing, of things slipping away. It was the dying fall of "Long ago."

While Jo was singing at Lilli's, Corrie had thought of Mum's funeral service, of sitting there with his whole attention concentrated on the daffodils in the vase on the table at the front of the church, shutting out everything else around him, thinking of Rousseau, falling waters, unpopulated greenness.

He was known to be a polite boy, respectful, well-mannered, shy. When people smiled at him, he smiled back, as though he were happy.

"He seems to be taking his mother's death very well," they said. "He's been so mature about the whole thing. Wonderful with Jo and Matthias."

How easily people can be fooled, he thought, not with pleasure, aware of depths within himself, little doors deep inside his head, doors that should never be opened.

Only Dad had seen him crying.

One night, two weeks after the funeral, he wanted to cry. He couldn't stop himself any longer. It was late at night, and he was scared that Jo—in the adjoining room—might hear him. He knelt down in the bathroom, with the light off, his head pressed down on the edge of the bath. Cool air rose from the plug-hole. The smell of Pears' soap. He watched a tear run down the side of the bath, like following raindrops down a window-pane, the rug pressing into his knees through his thin pyjamas, and then had to leave the bathroom because he was making a noise and Jo was just along the corridor.

He went downstairs, looking for somewhere to cry. Dad found him in the pantry, sitting on the bottom shelf beside

the bread-bin, his feet resting on the potatoes in the vege-
table rack, bent over, crying into a tea-towel smelling of
lemon-juice.

Dad stood in the doorway, in his dressing-gown, looked
at him for a moment, came inside, and they remained with
their arms around each other for a long time in the darkness. He never said a word the whole time, and never said
anything about it afterwards.

Dad hadn't been fooled.

Corrie had always felt that he would have been friends
with his Mum and Dad even if they hadn't been related.
Sometimes he called them by their first names, Pieter and
Margaret. They had both been twenty-one when he was
born. They were always ready to discuss his theories with
him, and always said "Thank you" if he did something for
them. When he was small—smaller—Dad used to give
him rides on his shoulder, and in the weeks after Mum's
funeral they seemed to go back to those times they had
together. Dad wrestled with him, lifted him up, threw him
into the air. It was a bit embarrassing at his age, but it was
nice. Dad gave him little jobs to do, and sat with him,
talking, side by side, as he painted, did the garden, or
sorted out the files in the office. One week they changed
round all the furniture in the house, and Dad let him
choose the new colours to repaint the downstairs rooms.
He took them all out in the car every week, and they
would talk about everything they'd seen. He left him
alone when he wanted to be alone. Dad had talked with
him about how much he missed Mum. When they were
in London—the time they had gone to see Lilli—Dad
had taken him and Jo to the National Gallery one morning, and pointed out to them the place where he and Mum
had first met, in front of "A Young Woman Seated at a

Virginal." Corrie still smiled inwardly to himself when-ever he saw a reproduction of this painting.

It was when he was outside alone that he felt the pres-sures of the outer world. He felt the weight of other people all around him. Every time he left the house, he had to prepare himself. A walk across the Green involved a need to greet and smile at half a dozen people. Because he was small and serious, adults often took it upon themselves to coax a smile out of him when he was alone with them. They all seemed to be taller than he was. He dreaded being alone with Mr. Arundel, the newsagent. He some-times longed for a shop where he could go in and not be known, just buy a magazine or a packet of sweets, as he could in that shop in Lowestoft, without the need for the smile, the greeting, a few polite enquiries, the need to be good-natured, nice, a brave and well-brought-up boy.

Over coffee, in any one of a dozen houses in Southwold, he would have been a subject of interest and concern. Women he hardly knew, who passed him in the street and said "Hello, Corrie," or "How's your grandmother," would be looking him up and down as they smiled and passed a few polite words. They would report back to each other in an interested, casual way, a subject for con-versation, well meant, wanting to help, but they would report back. *I saw Cornelius this morning. How is he now?*

"He seems to be taking his mother's death very well."
"He's been so mature about the whole thing."
"Wonderful with Jo and Matthias . . ."

WHEN Jo finished singing, they moved out towards Church Street to make their way back home.

Faintly, the voices had come out of the darkness and

across the emptiness, high and clear in the cold air, shrill little voices singing of hope and steadfastness. The fir-tree is a symbol of faith. It is always green, in summer, and in winter also, when it is snowing. It is noble and alone. It comforts and strengthens us.

5

HIS COPY of *Grimm's Fairy Tales* was an awkwardly large volume to read in bed. He had tried to read it lying on his side, but he had to use both hands to hold the book, it was so heavy, and his wrists ached painfully and gave way. He ended by sitting up in bed, the book opened against his upraised knees beneath the bedclothes, his music notebook lying on top of his school atlas on the bed beside him.

He looked at Lilli's illustration for "Hansel and Gretel" on the wall at the side of his bed, studying it as he often did, lying in bed before he went to sleep.

> DR. ERNST JACOBY
> *Berlin-Charlottenburg*
> > 24th November 1938

Dear Sir,

Please allow us to tell you about our position, and about our hopes. We hope you listen kindly to the situation in which we and our family find ourselves. Mrs. Katherina Viehmann has told us about your school, and about your kindness, and we have looked at your prospectus with great interest. We are friends of Mrs. Viehmann.

You know, dear sir, how matters stand with us in Germany, and since the events of this month the situation for Jews in this country is developing and becoming worse. We were compelled to give up our practices as doctors here, and, though it is now difficult to leave Germany without having a very particular reason for doing so, we hope to get government permission to emigrate to the United States. We need somewhere where our children will be able to continue their education and wait in safety while we try to carry out our plans. We ourselves make all efforts for leaving Germany, so that, within sight, the children could return in their father's house. It would also be good for them, for their English and for their health in the summer, because there are forbidden all the swimming-baths and all the parks.

We think our plans may take about a year to work. We do not know how long we will have to wait before we can leave the country, and, when we go to the United States, we do not think we could take the children with us, as it will be difficult for us at first to settle there and begin again.

We have three children: a girl of thirteen, a boy of twelve, and a girl of ten. They do not know any word of English, and if they learn well for a year, it will help them to settle in a school in America.

We have many questions to ask, which we hope do not trouble you.

Is it possible that you manage with our children, who do not know English? They know much, much less than Kurt and Thomas Viehmann when they first came to your school. Will it be too difficult for them with strangers in a foreign place? Is there, perhaps, a teacher who can speak German, so that, when, in the first time, they may feel unhappy, they would have someone who could listen to them? My wife and I speak English quite well, and we shall instruct our children so that they will have a little basis, and not feel so lonely if they can talk to their comrades. We will show them pictures so that England can become a place they can imagine. The oldest boy and girl

have learned French and Latin in their "Gymnasium." We
do not know, perhaps this will help to learn English for
them.

We are worried about the holidays, as the children will
have no home. The children, as Jews, can only have
passports which prevent them coming back to Germany
again. Where could they go? Could they stay in the
school? We know no one in England.

Your prospectus says the fee of 90L per annum. This
part is difficult for us to write. We have a severe loss over
the last five and a half years because of the situation here,
and we are limited in our money. We will be allowed to
leave Germany with a very little amount only, which we
need to begin a new life in America. If you would be able
to allow a special agreement for three children it would
be valuable to us. We think we would be able to spend at
the very maximum 20L per month for all the three
children. This payment will be safe when we are in
America, because whatever new restrictions are made on
the transfer of money from Germany this cannot be
affected. Until this time, the children's grandmother in
Warsaw, and a friend who is now living in Prague have
agreed to pay, though it will be difficult for them. We do
not think that we will be able to pay, ourselves, from
Germany. We know the difficulties that Mrs. Viehmann
had.

Need we buy new clothes for them, the uniforms and
the equipment, if they will be only in England for a year?
What should they bring in the way of suits and other
necessities? Do the boys generally wear long trousers?
What do they require for sport? Must they buy the
required English school-books already over here, or are
they supplied in the school? Would they be allowed to
wear ordinary clothes? It would be difficult for us to spend
the money on many new clothes. Their clothes are not

fashion clothes, but are suitable for children, and practical for school. Please excuse all these questions, but once the children are in England, they will have no money to buy anything.

If all works well, we hope our children can be at your school for the January term. When does the term begin? Could they stay somewhere before the term begins?

We hope you will listen to our questions with sympathy.

We ask you to tell us quite frankly whether you have any reason why you would prefer us not to send our children over. After recent events, you might see things from a different point of view, and we are anxious not to cause you or your school any difficulties. The position in Germany is such that we cannot make any firm promise to you about what might or what might not happen in the future, and the chances are that things will not turn better.

Our children are good and decent little people, and behave very well. You will not regret taking them into your school. Please don't mind the trouble we cause you. We love our country, but we must leave Germany.

> Yours sincerely,
> Dr. Ernst Jacoby and
> Dr. Madeleine Jacoby

HE OPENED *Grimm's Fairy Tales* again at "Hansel and Gretel," and then turned the pages back to "The Wolf and the Seven Little Kids," thinking of earlier that evening, when he was sitting on the step beside Jo, listening to Lilli reading. He had a reproduction of a Bewick woodcut as a book-plate in the book. Four little boys sat astride engraved and listing gravestones, riding them as though they were horses. They were dressed as soldiers.

He had just started rereading the story when he heard Jo moving about in his room next door. As he listened, he heard the school clock strike a single note, half past eleven, its deep note followed by the higher single chime of the restaurant clock. The music did not play on the half-hour. Jo and he were the only people in Tennyson's: Matthias was sleeping in Lilli's house.

There was a louder bang from the next room, a sound like the bed being shifted.

He wondered if Jo had had another nightmare, and then if he were suffering from asthma again. He had looked a little hunched-up earlier in the evening—the whole upper part of his body shrivelled in on itself—and had gone to bed early, about half an hour after they had arrived back from the churchyard.

He pulled his dressing-gown on and walked through into Jo's room.

The bedside light was on, and Jo was standing beside his bed, pulling at the bedclothes.

"Hello, little Cornelius."

"Hello, minuscule Johann."

"You got me all excited then. I thought Santa was coming back for a second visit."

"Have you done it again?"

Jo pulled a wry face, and nodded, indicating the wet sheets he was removing from the bed.

"Santa Claus had better wear wellies if he does call again." He began to sing, "I'm dreaming of a damp Christmas." At irregular intervals, he had started to wet his bed, and there was a settled routine to be gone through when it happened.

"You get rid of the sheets, Jo. I'll remake the bed for you."

"Perhaps I should have been trained with one of those musical potties. The ones that play a tune when you've produced something."

"I always thought they were a rather sinister idea."

66

"*Brave New Po.*"

"And I should think a lot would depend on the tune they chose."

"What if they chose the national anthem?"

"It could have disastrous consequences in later life. Just imagine, every time you heard that tune you'd . . ."

". . . burst with patriotic fervour."

"It could ruin a promising career in the diplomatic corps."

"It could ruin several dozen pairs of socks."

"And the dangers of a short circuit . . ."

"It doesn't bear thinking about."

The replies came rapidly, automatically. Jo could go on to automatic pilot, and carry on a conversation for a long time, with his mind completely absorbed elsewhere.

He had already washed himself and put on a dry pair of underpants. He slept in a T-shirt and underpants, the pants being easier to clean if he wet himself. He had a wide range of T-shirts with illustrations and slogans. The one he was wearing at the moment had "This Space to Let" printed on its front. He stood across the bed from Corrie as they bundled together the sheets and the waterproof cover. He always held himself very upright, like a small child being reprimanded, just as Corrie did.

"I thought you were putting up some Christmas decorations in here."

"I decided it was not in the nature of boys to do that kind of thing."

Jo walked out and went towards the bathroom as Corrie took the spare sheets from the shelf in the cupboard, left ready by Lilli. There was the sound of a tap being turned on.

Jo came back in as Corrie was smoothing out the bottom sheet on the mattress, and stood looking at him for a moment. Corrie smoothed and smoothed the bottom sheet until it was absolutely free of wrinkles. Jo replaced the pillow on the bed, and took the other side of the top sheet.

"Can you think of any uses for a blanket?" Corrie asked as they began to tuck one into the sides of the bed.

Mr. Passenger had asked Jo's class once to spend an English lesson in writing down as many different uses as they could think of for a barrel, a paper-clip, a brick, and a blanket. Jo had thought of 117 uses before time had run out. Corrie had seen his list later. *A barrel can be used to float over the Niagara Falls. You have to be inside it, though. N.B.(1) You can get famous this way. N.B.(2) You can also get killed. A barrel can be used for making go-karts and things like that. Boy scouts do this. Greggers is a boy scout, but I don't think he makes go-karts out of things. You had better ask him. Better still, I'll ask him, and the next time I do a piece of work for you I'll put at the top whether he does or not. You can laugh at a barrel. You can have a discussion group, and talk about barrels. You can ignore a barrel. You can roll your trousers up and climb inside a barrel, then roll down a hill, shouting "Cheese!" or something like that. (It needn't be "Cheese." You can shout whatever you feel like shouting.)* The suggestion that Corrie had liked best was that a brick could be a Bible for an atheist.

Working together, in silence, they finished making the bed.

"Look at this," Jo said, turning round and pulling down the waistband of his underpants as he climbed back into bed. "Age 7" was printed on the label in broad black lettering beneath the manufacturer's name. "Humiliating, isn't it?"

"It's no fun being a dwarf."

"I found a poem about you the other day. 'A Considerable Speck,' it was called."

"Oh yes. Robert Frost and I often went swinging on birches together, until he fell off and killed his parrot."

There was a long silence.

Jo sat up in bed arranging the sheets about him, like a child ill in bed in the middle of the day.

Corrie sat in the cane rocking-chair, pushing himself backwards and forwards. Jo's clothes were neatly folded on the trunk at the bottom of his bed. The front of the thin sand-coloured jacket he had changed into when they got back from the churchyard was covered in metal badges: "I Am 2." "Head Girl." "Netball Captain." The badge with Shakespeare's head and "Will Power" on it was from when they had gone to see the Royal Shakespeare Company in London, during a short holiday the previous year.

The painting Lilli had given to Jo, one of her illustrations for "The Six Swans," hung above his bed. The wall around the painting was covered by large blown-up black-and-white photographs of family and friends which Jo had taken and developed. His own face, and the faces of Dad, Mum, Matthias, Lilli, Sal, his cousins Michael and Lincoln, Judith, Cato, and many others regarded Corrie from across the bed. He thought of Lilli's dining-room, and the intense close-up examination of the faces of the many people in all the paintings. The baby's face in the painting Lilli had given Jo was at the very front of the picture as it lay in its cradle beside its sleeping mother, and the evil Queen, her face hidden by a looped curtain at the other side of the room, was walking towards the baby, her hands just beginning to lift up from her side. There was a full-length photograph Jo had taken of him directly opposite. He was wearing the high-heeled boots he wore to make

him look taller, and jeans, and his hands were thrust into
the slanting pockets of the hooded zip-front sweat-shirt he
was wearing. He was pulling a funny face.

He walked across the room.

"I pray you sit by us, and tell's a tale," he said, sitting
on the bed beside Jo.

"Merry or sad shall 't be?"

"As merry as you will."

"A sad tale's best for winter."

He looked at Jo's T-shirt.

There was a fashionable shop in London selling T-shirts
with the symbol of the Red Phoenix terrorists—the flame
and the fist—on them. In the music magazine that Cato
bought, next to an advertisement for teenage spots, Corrie had seen a special offer placed by a mail-order company
for T-shirts with a line of bullet-holes printed across the
front, to make it look as if the wearer had been machine-
gunned. The shirts could also be ordered with bullet-holes
printed on the back as well as the front, to look as if the
bullets had gone right through the wearer's body. This cost
fifty pence extra.

Jo looked ill, strained. There were dark lines under his
eyes.

"O.K.?" Corrie asked.

Jo nodded.

"I thought your asthma had started when I heard you
moving about."

He told Jo about Matthias standing like Rupert the
Bear, and they sat in silence for a while.

"Any more news about that school?"

Corrie shook his head. "No. They just said again that
they wanted the other terrorists released from prison before they'll set anyone free."

"And the government won't let anyone be released?"

Corrie nodded.

"Just the same."

"Just the same."

"They can't do as the terrorists want, can they?" Jo asked. "Release the prisoners? Because if they do, it'll happen again."

"It will anyway."

"How do you stop it happening in the first place?"

"You can't, can you?"

"The German government isn't going to negotiate, whatever happens."

"Do you think they'll storm the building?"

"It's the only thing they can do."

"The terrorists say they've got the children spaced out in different rooms. Imagine it in school here. Even if they got to one group in time, the other terrorists would have time to kill the children with them. They've got four whole classes. Nearly a half of the school. Could the army attack all the different rooms simultaneously?"

"Something's going to happen before long. Everyone seems to be co-operating. The Russians and East Germans haven't made any objections about all the troops being there. They've offered to help."

"They've already killed five people. They've just been holding on to all those children for all this time."

Jo flicked at the mobile hanging above his bed, a quick, angry action. "They found somewhere to fly to when they'd killed Mum."

Something cold brushed against Corrie's lips. It was one of the figures from the mobile. The eight silvery-metallic sea-gulls swooped and soared in the slightest current of air. He moved back, rubbing at his mouth.

Their newspaper, *The Guardian*, had said "17 KILLED IN AIRPORT ATTACK." A more popular tabloid had had the headline "GOOD FRIDAY MASSACRE," adding "ONE BRITON BELIEVED DEAD." That had been Mum. She had been returning from a conference in Rome, a discussion of recent research into cancer. There was still hope of a breakthrough in finding a cure. She had gone even though she was pregnant.

He had stared at the photographs in *The Guardian*: a man swabbing at a floor with a mop, two men carrying something in a blanket between them. When he was watching the news report of the shooting at the school that afternoon, he had leaned forward to see the body of the woman in more detail. He had wanted to see her face.

The usual clutter of extraordinarily assorted books lay on the carpet beside Jo's bed, around Corrie's feet: *The Little Prince, Kobbé's Complete Opera Book*, an American photographic magazine, *The Mouse and His Child*, a paperback edition of *Small Is Beautiful* ("There's a book here about us," he had said to Corrie when he bought it), an old school edition of *Emil and the Detectives*. His changes of subject-matter from day to day were unpredictable.

His school rough-work book was lying clipped to his drawing-board. It was covered with his tiny neat printing: *Open only in case of earthquakes, tornadoes (gale force, assorted debris zooming about), custard pouring from volcanoes, Martians turning into cheese(Camembert), giant bats chewing gum in discothèques, the bus population going green (with ivy, not envy), celebration of annual haircut of Cato Levi, Saturnalia getting divorced from Copernicus, undulations in oscillating rhythm on British Rail track (1st class only)....* A length of wood, club-shaped, lay alongside the drawing-board, next to his flute, with the same printing on it in black felt-tip pen at the thinner end. YOB BASHER. HOLD THIS END. *Groin*: 10 *points. Legs*: 3 *points. Head*: 25 *points. Arse*: 4 *points.* At one end of it a black circle was labelled *Self-destruction button.*

Corrie looked at it, then picked it up, waving it at Jo, and spoke in his most refined and sophisticated voice.

"I say, how frightfully childish!"

"Well, we are children," Jo said, quoting from *Emil and the Detectives*. He reached over the other side of the bed, away from Corrie, and pulled up his Winnie-the-Pooh, clutching it to him and sucking his thumb noisily. In one sudden movement, he slid beneath the bedclothes, until only his eyes were visible above the sheets.

The ceiling had been entirely covered with Charlie Brown strip cartoons, clipped from a Sunday newspaper colour magazine, bright primary colours of red, blue, and yellow. Corrie thought of the reproduction of Breughel's "Children's Games" hanging in the school sanatorium. He had seen it when he had gone to visit Cato, after his appendicitis operation. Mechanically, joylessly, like troops drilled in some repetitive movement, the swarming children filling the streets played their games, each compelled to act the part of a child. Not a single child was laughing, or even smiling. With intense seriousness and concentration, they performed all the actions expected of children, over and over again like clockwork figures, a wound-up toy. Unseen, in the distance, was a refuge, a place to which they could escape if only they realised it was there. Beyond the trees, beyond the river, open green fields stretched emptily away towards a wide horizon.

Beside Jo's bed was the light Corrie had thought of when he had seen the cake at Lilli's: a pottery model of the gingerbread house, made so that the light would shine through the windows of the house when it was switched on. The front was open, and miniature furniture inside was clearly visible: the table, the chairs, the tiled oven.

"Neely?"

"Yes, Jo-Jo?"

They were nicknames from early childhood, now used rarely, and half-jokingly.

"Tell me about Rousseau."

This had been the usual request when he had sat on Jo's bed when he was younger.

Rousseau was the name of the mythical land Corrie had invented with Jo three years ago. Dad had been working on the notes for his paperback edition of *Émile* when they had been trying to think of a name for their land. On the wall beside Jo's bed, alongside one of Lilli's posters for *The Winter's Tale*, was the large detailed map of Rousseau drawn in coloured inks by Jo. There were other posters on the far side of it: a photograph of the earth from space; a Peaceable Kingdom, the animals grouped around a standing lion; and the programme for the Victorian Evening. Corrie read the first lines.

> *Mama, Papa, Edmund, and young Albert*
> *invite you to attend*
>
> A GLITTERING SOIRÉE.
>
> *Poetry, prose, music, and drama of an unimpeachable*
> *moral tone, expressly for your delectation and edification.*
> Musicians:
> *Cello: Master C. Meeuwissen.*
> *Flute: Master J. Meeuwissen.*
> *Violin: Mrs. M. Meeuwissen.*
> *Pianoforte: Mr. P. Meeuwissen.*

Jo blew at the mobile, and the silver birds rose and fell, spinning above the bed.

"Wings soar in the silence."

"Birds float above the sea."

"Falling waters from the cliff-tops."

"Lonely Rousseau waits for me."

Jo grinned. "You remember exactly."

"I still go there sometimes."

On the edges of the world, hidden by mist, lapped by the waters of an undiscovered sea, is the uninhabited solitude of a green and distant island. The only sounds are the waterfalls, plunging down over rocks to the distant unprinted shore, and the faint cries of birds, wheeling and turning like white fragments borne up by the wind. . . .

It had become a real place to him, existing outside his own imagination, when he had looked at one of the art books at Lilli's, the Christmas they had stayed with her, and saw reproductions of paintings that were scenes from inside his own head—green leaf-fringed shadows in the depths of cool woods—and found that the painter's name was Rousseau. He could still write fluently and rapidly in the script and language they had invented for it.

"Wings soar in the silence."

They both watched the silver birds slowly steady themselves, and stop.

"Do you think Matty liked his present?" Jo asked.

"Yes. He made enough noise with it."

"It's just as well we had a German Christmas and opened all our presents on Christmas Eve. Someone told him about Father Christmas at play school, and he was a bit scared of it happening in the middle of the night."

"I don't blame him. How would you like a hairy old geezer coming into your bedroom when you're fast asleep?"

"Treading reindeer muck into your carpet. Anyway, if he goes off his present, I'll play with it instead."

Jo emerged from beneath the bedclothes and sat up beside Corrie.

"Corrie?"

"Mmm?"

Jo hesitated for a moment, looked at Corrie again, and then reached down under his bed, bringing up a flat, square parcel in a plastic bag from a record shop. He placed it carefully on his knees and smoothed his hands across the top of the bag, smoothing out all the wrinkles.

He spoke with his head down, looking at his hands moving across the thin plastic.

"This is Mum's Christmas present."

Corrie watched him.

"I bought it last January, when we were in London in the New Year. It was just the right thing, and I had to buy it then. The records she had had got scratched. I kept it hidden in the bottom of the wardrobe."

He looked up at Corrie, staring at him very closely.

"She's bound to have seen it, isn't she?"

"What did you get her?"

"The *Saint Matthew Passion*."

Jo dropped his gaze, staring down at the package on his knees again.

"You couldn't afford that, could you, Jo? That's four records."

"They were having a sale. In Oxford Street. That's why I had to get it then. They'd had an incendiary bomb, and the box and the booklet had been damaged. They were selling a lot of records and things off cheaply. You remember. . . ."

In the railway stations, and on the underground, were warnings not to touch unattended packages or bags, and to report them to staff. They had had their bags searched several times, in theatres and concert halls, museums and art galleries. When they had gone to see the Royal Shakespeare Company, a man sitting in front of Corrie had left during the performance, and he had seen a parcel still lying under his seat. He had said nothing to anyone, afraid of making a scene, causing a disturbance, and sat throughout the second half of the play—as Juliet sobbed, drank the drug, was lamented, as Romeo rode to Verona to join his bride in death, wept beside her body in a feasting presence full of light, as both Romeo and Juliet killed themselves, as the Montagues and Capulets were reconciled with tears over the bodies of their children—thinking only of the green Marks & Spencer carrier-bag lying on its side in front of him. Beneath the surface of everyday life, nothing was what it seemed, and mutilation could lurk beneath the commonplace: a car, a pillar-box, an unattended parcel, an envelope with unfamiliar handwriting. In nearby streets were the sounds of the sirens.

Jo slid the contents out of the plastic bag. He had made a new box to hold the four records, and, in water-colours, had painted a cover showing the road to Calvary. He had done it beautifully, copying the style of one of Lilli's paintings.

He had chosen the interior of a family house, rooms opening out into deeper rooms through open doors, each room represented in close detail. In the different rooms, glimpses of a family could be seen, dressed in the fashion of the 1930s: a woman sewing, a boy bent over a toy, a man peering through his spectacles at a book, a little girl stroking a cat. Through one of the windows—unseen by any of the family, a casual detail almost lost in the general pattern of the picture—a crowd in the street was watching someone who had fallen down. His feet were just visible beyond the edge of the window. A man, fully visible, was standing immediately above the fallen figure, his arm about to rise and bring a whip down upon him. The faces of the crowd were neither gleeful nor excited. They were just gazing blankly at an occurrence of events over which they had no control. One or two were smiling. A few were averting their eyes.

Jo ran his hand around the edge of the box.

It had been their mother's favourite of all Bach's works. It had been played at her funeral.

"She's bound to have seen it, isn't she? Isn't she, Corrie?"

The school clock began to strike midnight. They both listened until it had finished and the echoes died away. The bells of the clock above the restaurant chimed, and then began to play their folk-song.

"Happy Birthday, Jesus."

"Happy Christmas, Jo."

"*Fröhliche Weihnachten*, Corrie. I enjoyed Lilli's German Christmas."

6

"**F**OOL!" said the woman. "If we do not do this, then all four of us will die of hunger. We must destroy them in order to live ourselves. Otherwise you might as well start making the coffins for us all now."

The man's heart grew heavy, and he would not agree with her. She did not leave him alone until he had agreed to her plan. He said to himself, "It is not right," and yet he agreed.

Hansel and Gretel, tormented by hunger, had been awake all this time, and had heard everything that their father and stepmother had said about them.

Gretel wept bitterly, and said to Hansel, "They do not want us. We cannot live when we're all alone in the world."

"Don't be frightened, Gretel," Hansel said. "I'll think of a way to save us both. I'll always be here to look after you."

When the adults were asleep, Hansel got up, put on his coat, and tiptoed downstairs. Very quietly, he opened the front door, and went outside. The moon was shining brightly, and the white pebbles which were scattered on the ground in front of the house glimmered in the moonlight like newly polished silver coins on the dark earth. Hansel bent down, and began to gather up the pebbles, dropping them into the pockets of his coat until they were both crammed full.

Then he went back into the house, closed the door very

quietly, and tiptoed upstairs, where Gretel lay waiting for him, frightened to be alone.

"God will not forsake us," Hansel said to Gretel. "Don't believe that we can ever be totally abandoned. Sleep peacefully, my dear little sister."

CORRIE sat on the window-seat in the first-floor bedroom at the back of the school music rooms, holding the postcards from Katherina Viehmann, and Peter and Aline Goetzel. The door set into the wall was open, and piles of carefully stacked papers were on the floor at his feet. He was leaning over, reading "Hansel and Gretel" from the *Grimm's Fairy Tales* lying open on the window-seat beside him, next to his music notebook, on top of his atlas. It was the afternoon of the twenty-eighth of December, his birthday.

He had always written music, increasingly so over the past two years, short pieces to be performed by the Elizabethan World Picture, or by his family, and he had written songs for Levi's, the group formed by Cato Levi. (Cato kept reminding him that his grandfather Michael Meeuwissen had compiled the classic *Folk Songs of Europe*.) After the success of Corrie's music for *The Winter's Tale*, Mr. Passenger, the teacher who had produced the play, asked him, during the party after the last night, if he had ever thought of writing the music for an original opera or musical to be performed in school.

That was all he had said, but it had stayed in Corrie's mind.

Just after the end of term, he had been lying in bed one night, his eyes upon the "Hansel and Gretel" painting.

There was something he felt a need to express about those two figures.

"Hansel and Gretel" moved and affected him deeply—

it was a story he had read and reread as a small child, and in the last few months—and he felt that he wanted to convey what he felt the story was trying to say, the atmosphere of Lilli's painting. It had been a mood, rather than a clear conception of what he might do, like the struggle for the words to describe a vivid but half-forgotten dream.

It had come to him that he might be able to express his feelings through music.

Over the past week he had started to sketch out ideas for a musical adaptation of the story. He wanted to make it free of the kind of inaccuracies he had seen in previous adaptations. Unlike the Humperdinck opera, there would be no caring parents, no Sandman, no Dew Fairy, no guardian angels.

Berlin-Charlottenburg

14.X.1935

Dear Mr. High,

Please send me a prospectus of your school. I write having received the best recommendation of Your school by Mrs. Viehmann, my dear friend, who I know since years. I must send my two children from Germany, a boy of twelve, and a girl of ten. As German Jew I have to select the Institut not only for the study, but I am forced to seek a school, the fees of which are corresponding to my reduced capital. I am a woman author, and my husband is a lawyer. We are both since 2 years without possibility of earn money. I hope You understand my incorrect English.

Yours faithfully,
Ruth Grünbaum

W H E N he first opened the door set into the wall in the music rooms, his ideas started to take shape. The mood had crystallised and the structure had begun to emerge: a cantata, with a narrator, a chorus, and mime, rather than a conventional operatic or musical treatment. "Auf meines Kindes Tod" was to be the final song for the chorus.

HE PICKED up his bookmark in *Grimm's Fairy Tales*, and looked again at Nickolaus Mittler's postcard:

> . . . Please pardon me about my stammerings, but my will is stronger than the words I know. We will be diligent in our study and becomingness, and prove ourselves worthy. We will be good boys. . . .

The music rooms, some distance behind Dunwich Green and the rest of the school buildings, were in the Ferry House, an early-Victorian building, away from the main built-up area of the little town. It had been the original headmaster's house until Tennyson's, on the east side of the Green, backing on to the low cliff above the beach, was built in the time of the third headmaster. Passers-by who walked along the western boundary of the school fields, down the footpath which led from the town towards the ferry across the River Blyth, often heard confused fragments of music as they passed the Ferry House in term-time.

His favourite room for practice was a first-floor room at the back of the building, looking out across the school playing-fields towards the sea, beyond the wall and the low sand-dunes. It had originally been one of the bedrooms in the house, high-ceilinged, tall-windowed, beautifully proportioned, with an ornate white-painted fireplace curly with leaves and bunches of grapes. He would borrow the key from his father—it helped, sometimes, to be the headmaster's son—and spend hours there during the long

holidays, when all the boarders had gone home, and there
was no one there to disturb him, bent over his cello, at the
piano, or just sitting in the cold bare room, above the
quiet, wall-enclosed fields.

O N T H E morning of Christmas Eve, sitting no the win-
dowseat of the practice room, he had looked down at Jo
acting as goalkeeper for Matthias on the First Eleven football pitch. Immediately after breakfast, he and Jo had
spent an hour or so together in the Ferry House, practising
"Auf meines Kindes Tod" and the other musical pieces they
were going to perform for the German Christmas. Jo kept
making spectacular and carefully unsuccessful attempts to
save the goals that Matthias kicked in from six feet away.
Matthias, knees bent, had to pump his arms up and down
to keep his balance, and occasionally fell flat on his face.
He was encrusted in mud, and the fine drizzle of the early
morning was intensifying into rain. Baskerville hung un-
certainly about in the background, occasionally making
hesitant little forays towards them.

Usually, his father gave him the single key to open the
door of the Ferry House when he wanted to go there to
practice in the holidays. But this day Corrie took the complete bunch of Ferry House keys from the office, without
bothering to remove the one key he usually used.

After practising his cello for two hours, he sat on the
window-seat jingling the bunch of keys in his hand, spinning them round on the ring.

Set in the wall of the bedroom was a locked door, a
panelled white-painted door with a brass handle.

On the key-ring was a little key he had not seen before.

He moved away from the window, and up to the inset
door.

He considered just walking past it, but he was drawn on

by curiosity. It was a door like any other. It was a key like any other key. He put the key in the keyhole, turned it only a little, and the door was open.

Beyond the bedroom door he stepped into darkness.

He stood for a moment until his eyes became accustomed to the dim light. It was a long, narrow, windowless room, like a boarded-over railway carriage. Slatted wooden shelves stretched away against the walls on both sides, stacked with dusty files of old incoming school mail.

The floor was white with the spilled contents of files which had fallen.

He squatted down in the dusty darkness, disappointed, mildly interested, picking up the letters lying nearest to him on the bare boards, letters from the late 1930s, letters about the trivial important concerns of childhood: a boy to have milk in his cocoa, a boy not to have eggs, discovered smokers, requests for details of entrance to the school, a new school heating system, an accident to a boy in a games lesson, the payment of fees.

Then, idly sifting through the papers at his feet, like the valueless litter left in an abandoned room, he came across the first of the letters which made him pause. From the window-seat above the playing-fields, he heard his brothers' voices sharp in the air around him.

Doors began to open, deep inside his head.

MINISTRY OF LABOUR

July, 1939

MILITARY TRAINING ACT, 1939.

I am directed by the Minister of Labour, in pursuance of the powers conferred upon him by Section 10 of the Military Training Act, to request that you will be good enough to furnish a return of information required by him with respect to certain persons who have attended your school.

Persons of whom information is required. The return should relate to all boys born between the 4th June, 1918, and the 3rd June, 1919, both days included, who have been on the school roll in your school at any time during the last five years.

Information to be included in the return. The particulars desired to be furnished in respect of each boy are:— full name, date of birth, home address and name of parent or guardian.

Form of return. It is desired that the particulars should be furnished upon cards which will be supplied to you for the purpose. One card should be used for each individual. A postcard form is enclosed upon which you are requested to notify to the Registrar General, Somerset House, London, W.C., the number of cards estimated to be required for the return. On receipt of the postcard, the requisite supply of cards will be forwarded to you.

I would add, after our earlier correspondence, that this return is asked for, not as an act of voluntary co-operation, but as a statutory duty imposed by Section 10 of the Military Training Act. A refusal to comply with the Minister's request would thus constitute a breach of the provisions of the law.

CIVILIAN PROTECTION LTD.
Warwick Plain, Coventry

8th June, 1939

Dear Sir,

We are pleased to be able to offer the supply of the following for the use and protection of the pupils under your control.

(i) IDENTIFICATION DISCS. The sensible suggestion has been made that the civilian population should have some readily available means of identification about them. We believe that, for children, the best possible method is the wearing of one of our clearly printed METAL IDENTIFICATION DISCS. Each disc can bear the name of the pupil and the school, and will be a great advantage to you in identifying your pupils quickly in case of any difficulties encountered as a result of an air-raid.

(ii) STRETCHERS. Our models are constructed of metal and fold easily for storage. There is no canvas to become discoloured or rot, and they may readily be hosed down if they become contaminated.

Our prices are most reasonable. The stretchers, for example, cost only 48/- each, but there is a considerable reduction if you place an order for more than a dozen.

We respectfully await your instructions.

Yours faithfully,
J. L. Carter,
Sales Manager

EMERGENCY COMMITTEE FOR THE
CARE OF GERMAN JEWISH CHILDREN
Rachel House, London W.1

11th July 1938

Dear Anthony High,

You have done so much for our children, that I hesitate to burden you any further, but you will realise the desperate urgency of the situation in Germany. Perhaps the Evian Conference will be able to find a solution, but we have hundreds of people who just cannot wait longer. There has been an enormous rise in applications for help. I am sure that you yourself will have become aware of this from Leonie Matthias in Berlin.

Please forgive me if I ask you to please give me a brief indication of any further help you feel able to offer. Have you room for any children at all in September? Do you specify any particular ages? How many boys could you take? Could you take any more girls? What is the lowest possible figure you would be willing to accept as fees? (As you know, it is virtually impossible to get any money out of Germany.) Would you be willing to allow me to act on your behalf in accepting any children? I give you my assurance that the Committee and I will make the fullest investigation of each case.

We are keenly aware of the generosity of yourself and your Committee, and you may feel that you have done all you could be reasonably expected to do, but we hardly know where to turn, and we need to get as many children out of Germany as possible, and as quickly as possible. Each place offered would mean that one more child was safe.

I would be very grateful if you could reply soon. With renewed thanks.

Yours sincerely,
Hannah Greif

Below him, on the football pitch, Matthias and Baskerville had seemed to hit upon a co-ordinated plan. Jo did a complete back-somersault over Baskerville, and nearly ended up with his head jammed beneath the net. "You're supposed to be the referee!" he complained fiercely. "Canine nutter!" Matthias began to dance about because he had scored, moved more quickly than his legs could keep up with, and fell over. The high clear voices floated up from the field, and Corrie felt the vague, powerful forces of the adult world beginning to gather, waiting, at the edges of childhood, unseen by the children.

The next thing he picked up was the postcard from Nickolaus Mittler, posted on the twentieth of June, 1939.

He spent the rest of the morning trying to sort his way through the massed and scattered papers on the floor in the inner room, arranging them slowly in different piles that approached some rough chronological order. On the afternoon of Christmas Day, he left the others watching *The Wizard of Oz* on television. Dorothy had just started to follow the yellow brick road. On each day since then, he had come down to the Ferry House, saying that he was going to practise his cello. Patiently, carefully, he had tried to trace his way through the files of correspondence, beginning in 1933. The flimsy yellow papers were like documents from centuries ago, unfamiliar moustached or bearded figures on faded stamps with tiny denominations.

He knew that the school had been evacuated during the war, and the staff and children moved away, when Southwold had been declared a prohibited area. The records for the 1930s and 1940s were disorganised and incomplete, and a good number of the 1930s files—whole stretches between 1934 and 1938—seemed to have been lost or destroyed.

There were three files for each year—heavy box files with rusted metal clips inside—usually exactly divided into four-month periods, but some were unsorted random piles of documents from different years bundled together, damaged by fire, scorched or partially burned. In all the files, and strewn about the floor, in increasing numbers as the years went by, were the many letters from Jewish families in Germany, a part of the past of Lilli, and of himself.

It was difficult, with the incompleteness and confusion of the files from the dark inner room, to follow through the correspondence of individual families over the years— some names just seemed to vanish, and with others it was unclear whether or not children had actually managed to get to the school—but as he approached the final file of late 1939, he had got to know some of the families well. Intent, absorbed, he read on, unable to draw himself away, as the letters and postcards poured in from Berlin, month after month, sometimes couched in the awkward English of commercial communications, asking if there was any possibility of a vacancy at the school: ordinary men and women, mothers and fathers, decent people, trying to learn how to plead, for themselves, and for their children.

H E P L A C E D the two postcards on the window-seat in front of him, side by side.

> *Berlin-Charlottenburg 4*
> 15th May 1934
>
> Dear Sir, I would be happy if you could please be so kind to send me a prospectus of your school. I was given your address by Miss Leonie Matthias, "Elternhilfe für die jüdische Jugend." My boys whom I want to send to England are 10 years old and 13 years old. They have some knowledge of English, and can understand when people speak English to them, but they cannot really speak. More than 60L each for a year I cannot devote to my boys' education. I know it is a small sum. We are Jews. Will this mean difficulties in the school with their comrades? We are not political, and do not belong to any organisation. We have a great desire to give our sons under your care.
>
> Yours faithfully,
> Frau Katherina Viehmann

> *Berlin-Charlottenburg 2*
> 18th January 1938
>
> Dear Mr. High,
> I need an attestation for the german authorities that my daughter Charlotte Goetzel is going to Southwold School. Please send me this paper in the next days.

Lotte cannot speak English and it is the first time that
she is separated from her home and from her parents. She
is our only child. Please treat her with great love and
solicitude. Please, if you have a little time, let us know
whether you are content with her.

Thank you for your kind help in our bad circumstances.

With sincere good wishes,
Peter and Aline Goetzel

He turned the two postcards over, and again studied the
sepia photographs carefully.

*Blick vom Hotel Adlon auf den Pariser Platz; im Hin-
tergrund Tiergarten, Siegessäule, Reichstag, Berlin. (Sight
from the Hotel Adlon on the Parisian Place; in the background the Tiergarten, column of victory, parliament-
building, Berlin.)*

The Brandenburg Gate, with its six banks of neo-classical columns, the triumphal arch at the start of Berlin's
major central thoroughfare, seemed like a gate in Roman
times, a clear boundary between the city and the countryside. In front of the Gate, the wide empty expanse of the
start of Unter den Linden stretched away. On the right,
buildings were crammed together, as though crowded
within the walls of an over-populated and rapidly growing
city, the square towers and shallow central dome of the
Reichstag rising above everything else. Behind the Gate,
as though it were wild and open countryside, were the
trees of the Tiergarten. Beyond these was Charlottenburg,
and the other fashionable western suburbs, safe, middle-
class, comfortable. From amongst the trees of the Tiergarten, Victory rose up on her column, and above the Gate
another figure of Victory, in a chariot pulled by four
horses, faced down Unter den Linden.

The photograph on the second postcard—*Reichstags-gebäude und Brandenburger Tor, Berlin. (Parliament-building and Brandenburger Gate, Berlin)*—showed a wide empty avenue, leafless trees, and, opposite the massive frontage of the Reichstag, the Brandenburg Gate, its columned frontage facing the entrance to a bridge. The Gate appeared to be a solid structure with no way through.

The same buildings appeared over and over again in all the postcards: shifting angles, changing viewpoints, the same immense structures blocking the sky.

ON CHRISTMAS DAY, in one of the surviving files for 1933, he found the first letter from Rachel House, and then, soon afterwards, all the others.

EMERGENCY COMMITTEE FOR THE
CARE OF GERMAN JEWISH CHILDREN
Rachel House, London W.1

19th July 1933

Dear Mr. High,

Do you remember me from fifteen years ago, when we both served on the Stewart-Hamill Committee? I remember you (and Mrs. High) well, and how pleased you both were because David had just started to speak. (Yes, it was a long time ago!) I remember, also, how, as a result of the findings of this Committee, you were so ready to give free places to five of the starving Austrian children, and how you felt that the happiness that resulted was as great for you as it was for them.

We are just one of many agencies and organisations endeavouring to help German refugees—pacifists, professional people, Jews, evangelicals, etc.—but our particular concern, as our name indicates, is with German Jewish children. I realise that we are certainly not unique in this field, and I am afraid that the number of agencies so concerned will increase rapidly and inevitably if the current situation in Germany intensifies. I do hope that I can presume on a previous acquaintanceship to seek your help. Here at Rachel House we are trying to help refugee Jewish children whose parents are in concentration camps, or deprived of their means of livelihood. We have established close contact with a Jewish organisation in Berlin (Miss Leonie Matthias, "Elternhilfe für die jüdische Jugend," Berlin-Charlottenburg, Tiergartenstrasse), and hope to work together to alleviate the suffering caused by the actions of the present German government.

Could you take two or three of these children in September? Even a tentative promise "subject to the approval of the School Committee" will be helpful. Are there other headteachers in your area who might also be willing to help, with boys or girls? Would you be able to offer places to girls at your school? (We hope to keep brothers and sisters together.) I will be happy to supply you with any further details, or answer any questions.

I hope that you will feel able to help.

Yours sincerely,
Hannah Greif

DR. WILHELM VIEHMANN
Berlin-Charlottenburg 4

23rd September 1934

Dear Mr. High,

Thank you very much for your letter from last week. My husband found the week he spent in England when he brought our boys a very happy time. He has told me all about Southwold, and about meeting you and your family.

The start of life in England, and the beginning of term

in a new school, have been very great events for our boys, and Kurt and Thomas write very much in their letters about it, and show a happiness they have not known for many months. Their letters talk much of their sport-life, and I am very glad that they are involved in this traditional "fair sport" side of English manner of life.

Kurt is beginning to imitate the English orthography, and he does progress. He is beginning to write the nouns with the small letters in the correct way. He is telling me he is knowing the language "jolly well." Thomas, I think, is a little homesick. He is gentler in mind than Kurt, and more longing for tenderness. Everyone he knows in the world is in Germany. I hope that he will accustom more and more to your life and will be a good comrade among the other boys. Are you satisfied with their progress in English, and with their behaviour?

I hope my husband tried to tell you how thankful we both are that our boys are in your school during this difficult time and learn all about English life, but he does not speak English well. *My* English is not enough to express to you all the thankfulness we feel towards you and your school. I could not express it in German. You hardly know what a relief it is for us in our situation that our children are taken care of in your community, where they can be children, without the troubles of the adult world. I am so grateful that, with comrades of their own age, they will perhaps forget soon what they were compelled for so many months to endure, with the sorrows of grown-up people, the many conflicts and pains they have suffered in their native country. With a heavy heart we sent them away, but we feel comforted knowing you care for them in our bad times. It is a marvellous experience in our life to find friends in a country where we are only strangers. People are kind. We must remember this.

With many thanks for all your kindness towards us
and our children. Kindest regards, also, to Misses High,
please. The boys' grandmother, also, sends her good
wishes.

> Yours thankfull,
> Frau Katherina Viehmann

Please give my love to my boys. I wait for their Sunday
letters. I hope their colds are better.

> *London W.C.1*
> 22nd Oktober 1935

Very respected Mr. High,

I have heard of your school through my friend Kurt
Viehmann who has been a pupil at your school since one
year, who ask you that I please would be accepted also.

I am 14 years old, a German Jew, as Kurt is. I went
in Berlin to the same "Gymnasium" as Kurt, and you may
ask there a report about me. I was good student. I have
my school reports with me here in England, and can show
them to you. My wish is to be a physician.

My parents' letter will arrive soon. They told me to
ask you if I could be allowed in your school. They have
told me that if I can find a school to take me, I need not
go back to Berlin. Please let me come to your school, Mr.
High. I beg to ask that you will accept me. My parents
will not be able to afford that I come to England a second
time. My fees will be paid monthly, which you will
receive directly from my uncle in Paris, in French francs.

I am already one week in London, and my permission
to remain in this country is soon expiring. I soon must
return to Berlin if I find no school. You would oblige me
very much if you let me know your decision soon.

> Yours respectfully,
> Rudolf Seidemann

P.S. Please deliver my best regard to Kurt. Thank you.

EMERGENCY COMMITTEE FOR THE
CARE OF GERMAN JEWISH CHILDREN
Rachel House, London W.1
7th February 1936

RE: *Kurt and Thomas Viehmann.*

Dear Anthony High,

I was in Berlin over the New Year, and I'm afraid that
the extraordinarily stringent financial restrictions operated
by the German authorities are going to lead to some
heartbreaking situations. Thousands of German refugees
are going to find it virtually impossible to get help, or to
leave the country. Life is made unbearable for them, so
that they are driven to make arrangements to leave the
country, and then it is made so difficult for them that they
are unable to carry out their plans.

I saw Kurt and Thomas's mother, and no one could be
more full of gratitude than she is for you and Southwold,
and what you are doing for her sons. Her only comfort in
her current situation is to know that they, at least, are safe
in England.

But we don't know what we can do about the school
fees. When they sent their boys to England in 1934, they
felt sure that they knew of a safe and permanent way to
get money out of Germany to pay the boys' fees, but they
now realise that they were mistaken. Things have tightened
up fiercely. They have tried every possible way to transfer
money to England, but, of course, they have no relations
outside Germany who could help them.

They thought, at one stage, of your finding English
people who were going to travel for holidays in Germany,
and who would need German currency for their stay. You
could have given these tourists their address in Berlin,
and a slip with your signature, and they would have given
the money for the fees to these people, who would repay

you in English money when they returned home. Just before this happened, the boys could have written home to tell their parents that friends were going to visit them from England to give them the latest news from school, informing them of their names, to act as a safeguard. I felt that this was really too dangerous a plan.

Another idea they had considered recently was to support a German child in need—chosen by a British charity in Berlin—and to arrange for an equivalent sum to be transferred via the charity to England to pay for the boys' school fees: but this would not have been permitted, as I had to point out. Their final idea—and they really are desperately anxious to fulfil their commitment—is to have English children staying as their guests in Berlin for some time, if the children's parents would agree, in exchange, to pay for the fees of Kurt and Thomas. I understand that when the boys returned home for the Christmas holidays, Kurt brought an English schoolfriend home with him, and they showed him all the sights of Berlin, and he had a very enjoyable time. Is there any possibility of this working?

If not, the Viehmanns will be quite unable to pay the boys' school fees.

There are going to be many more similar cases, where children do not have relations outside Germany willing to pay for them. What can we do? The clearing systems are totally inadequate for the huge volume of finance which should be passing through for school fees. We have such limited resources, and so many cases on our books, that the Committee have decided that we cannot possibly accept any new cases under any circumstances for the payment of fees through the Exchange Clearing. We, therefore, will be unable to offer any financial assistance for Kurt and Thomas Viehmann, and have told Mr. and Mrs. Viehmann of the failure of their plans.

You might feel that the only possible answer is that the
boys must be sent back into Germany, as you can hardly
justify their staying on at your school, but I know that
you will be fully aware of the effect of this news on Kurt
and Thomas. I know what it is like for Jewish children in
Berlin schools. I am so very sorry.

Yours sincerely,
Hannah Greif

DR. WILHELM VIEHMANN
Berlin-Charlottenburg 4
15th February 1936

Dear Mr. High,

I have heard the news from "Elternhilfe für die
jüdische Jugend" about the news from the "Rachelhouse."
I do not want you to believe that our non-paying is
deliberate. It is for us a matter of course and honour to
pay the fees as soon as the German regulations will allow
this. We do not know what to do. Yesterday I walked to
see Mrs. Kirchner, who I know wrote to you about her
two children, and said she was aided by the Clearing-
House of "Elternhilfe" for paying her fees. I wished to
discover how she had succeeded so well. But I was sad
when her statements were vague, and found she was only
pretending. Mrs. Kirchner is only on the waiting-list, just
as I am. I do not blame her for what she said. She had
been told that her son Alex's turn had come (after
eighteen months waiting) and then they announced to
her that they were doing nothing for boys under fourteen.

I applied again to "Elternhilfe" for news of my position
on the waiting-list for the Clearing-House for the money,
and hope to hear a clear answer by next week. I hope that
then we shall be able to transfer a sum of money to pay the
money we owe you soon. It is difficult for us now to travel
to England, since we have lost our German citizenship.

We are very gratefull for all you have done for our boys. You have given them back their bright childhood, and made it possible for them to build up their lives. Please trust us, Mr. High. We shall do all we can to pay the money. Please excuse the trouble we are obliged to arise. I ask if you will allow our boys to remain in your school. You understand I would not ask if I would not be obliged to do so. We have caused you so many worries and difficulties.

Thank you for all your help to Kurt and Thomas, and to us.

Affectionately yours,
Katherina Viehmann

Aliens Department   *Home Office, Whitehall*

4th April 1936

With reference to your letter of the 26th March, I am directed by the Secretary of State to say that he regrets that he is not prepared to entertain an application for the grant of a certificate of naturalization to Kurt Erich Viehmann during his minority.

I am, sir,
Your obedient Servant,
J. Dickinson

Berlin-Charlottenburg 2
5th April 1938

Dear Mr. High,

Only today we got a letter from Lotte which rather afraid us. It is, we think, a little lonely for her by herself in the holidays. She seems to feel so lonely and homesick, and thinks she has no friends. She misses, also, her little dog. She seems to weep every night, and we worry about our dear daughter. She writes absolutely unhappy in the idea not to get through the examination! Lotte feels so anxious about the Mathematics. We hope that this is only a nervousness of hers. Were you satisfied with the results of her report-book? She tells us that the doctor told her she should swim and lead an active life, and not worry too much about herself.

Lotte tells us that no payment has reached you from my brother in Palestine. Please remember him if by mistake a payment should be late. I wrote to my brother with this sense, and he says it would only be on account of the difficulties in sending, but he is sure he will be able to manage it. If there are any questions of this kind, please, dear Mr. High, do not tell the child about them. Lotte feels very upset.

The 15th April is Lotte's birthday. Would you kindly buy her a little chocolate? It is almost impossible for us to send it abroad. We want to help Lotte, but we feel so helpless.

Excuse, please, these problems.
Peter and Aline Goetzel

Berlin-Charlottenburg
15th June 1939

Dear Sir,

Mrs. Greif did write to Miss Matthias from England and tell me the acception of me and my big brother as pupils of your school next term at a fee of £55 p.a. which enable us to fulfil our one wish to continue with our learning and our music. My father will send you the Form and Application for Admission. I only wish to thank you for your extreem kindness.

Yours very grateful,
Nickolaus Mittler

The photograph on the other side of Nickolaus Mittler's first postcard was an aerial view of Berlin Cathedral. Corrie had never known that Berlin had had a cathedral.

A C O L D wind was blowing down a broad street lined with balconied apartments. Most of the shutters were closed, and all the doors were locked.

He saw a lonely face at a window.

Inside a second-floor apartment, Nickolaus Mittler was slowly, patiently, writing at a table near the window, bent over, intent. Loose papers, postcards, books, and dictionaries were around him. The boy wrote and wrote, card after card, the pen-nib scratching in the silence of the room. Behind him, in the corner of the room, beside the window, her head turned towards it, a woman stood very still, as though listening for a sound outside in the street. In the hall, packed suitcases were lined against the wall. The suitcases were expensive, but the hall was empty of furniture and the walls were bare. A man and an older boy sat on the uncarpeted boards of the floor, beside the telephone. They were all wearing their best clothes.

Behind the four still, rapt figures, open doors led through to other doors, deeper inside, other rooms, other lives, just out of sight, closed doors opening deeper and deeper inside.

7

DURING his early lessons with Lilli after her stroke, he had made use of his school atlas, giving her the names of places—Dresden, Berlin, Southwold, King's Lynn, London—she had to find and point out to him. On page fourteen both parts of Germany were coloured the same pale orange colour, as though the country were whole and it was the time before the war.

Lilli's finger poised in the air above the open atlas, moved down—Spandau, Potsdam, Brandenburg, Charlottenburg—and came firmly to rest upon Berlin.

Berlin, like Vienna to the south of it, was so enormous a city that it was not represented, even on the small-scale map of the school atlas, as a dot or a square, but as an irregular solid area of grey to show the extent of the built-up area. Charlottenburg, where the Viehmanns and Nickolaus Mittler lived, where so many of the Berlin letters and postcards came from, was a large western suburb of Berlin, a circle as large as any independent town at the edge of the vast unknown city.

HE HAD a picture in his mind of Germany in the early 1930s, before the bombs started falling, before all the millions of people were led away into the darkness, a picture made up from books he had read, films and television documentaries he had seen.

In the countryside lived girls called Heidi, with braided

blonde hair, who stood on the mountainsides with their hands on their hips, smiling, in dazzlingly bright sunshine. They wore white blouses with big puffed sleeves, little white embroidered aprons, and lace-up bodices like the one that the Walt Disney version of Snow White wore. Unlike Snow White, they had big breasts. Every mountainside was crowded with big-breasted blonde girls with their hands on their hips, simpering at the camera. All the men were called Fritz and wore leather shorts, and little hats with feathers in them. They carried big ornate beer steins in their right hands, and sometimes they yodelled. Behind them were their brightly painted wooden houses, exact copies of the weather-houses and cuckoo clocks that were made inside them. Heidi and Fritz smiled and smiled in the bright sunshine, and tried to look like reality in the brightly coloured posters in the travel agencies all over the world. Their teeth were very white.

The mountains encircled the plain, and between the mountains and the plain were the forests, surrounding it on every side. The forests were very dark, and the trees were fir-trees, immensely tall. It was possible to see only a yard or so into the forest, into the blackness, and there was no grass. It would be terrifying to be lost in that darkness in which nothing grew. The mountains and the plain and the forest were the countryside. At the centre of the plain was the city. Long straight roads converged across the flat bleak plain towards the city. They were not tree-lined. Tree-lined roads were French.

Germany was the city, and the city was called Berlin.

The picture he had in his mind was in black and white. He could not imagine a colour picture of Germany in the 1930s.

"I am sure that he will like Berlin. It's a city made for children."

That was what Frau Wirth, the baker's wife, had said to Emil's mother, Frau Tischbein, bending over a basin as she had her hair washed.

"What a din the traffic made! Why, there were streets which are just as brightly lighted at night as during the day."

The motor cars rushed past the tram honking and squealing, signalling right and left turns, swinging round corners, while other cars followed immediately behind them. How noisy the traffic was! And there were so many people on the pavement as well! And from every side street came delivery vans, tramcars, and double-decker buses! There were newspaper stands at every corner, and wonderful shop-windows filled with flowers and fruit, and others filled with books, gold watches, clothes, and silk under-wear. And how very, very tall the buildings were.

So this was Berlin.

It had already grown dark. Electric signs flared up everywhere. The elevated railway thundered past. The underground railway rumbled and the noise from the trams and buses and cycles joined together in a wild con-cert. Dance music was being played in the Café Woerz. The cinemas in the Nollendorf Square began their last per-formance of the evening. And crowds of people pushed their way into them.

"Berlin is wonderful, of course," Emil continued, *"but I'm not so sure that I'd like to live here always. Just imagine what would have happened to me if I hadn't found all of you, and were quite alone here. It scares me even to think of such a thing."*

AS FAR as the eye could see, the hundred thousand streets and squares of the immense sprawling baroque city stretched on and on to the horizon in every direction. It was a cold, bleak city, the third largest city on earth, a grey city of stone façades and neo-classical pillars and columns. Massive stone official buildings, bleak, formidable, on a larger-than-human scale, stretched down broad triumphal ways, their frontages inset with many balconies and steep-set small-paned windows, their surrounds encrusted with curly decorative scrolls and ornate shields, and the figures of gods and goddesses. Wires crossed from side to side of wide boulevards, suspending lamps and traffic-lights, and cables for trolleys. Tram-lines stretched away like curves left by skaters in ice, down streets traced with the slim graceful columns of lampposts, elaborate filigree metal curls, lamps suspended like pendants from their arched tops. Opera houses, theatres and concert halls, churches, and government buildings lined the main streets, raising domes, spires, and pillars high into a low sky from which rain was falling.

The great crowds spilled across the streets, beneath the trees and the domes and the spires. The streets were wide and bordered by trees, and the crowds thronged them at all hours of the day and night, spilled out of trolley-cars, strode briskly across the tram-lines, passed the packed terraces of outdoor cafés, filled the roads so that only the tops of cars showed, strolled through parks with formal gardens and playing fountains, sheltered from the rain under the trees as boys in sailor suits watched model yachts on rain-pocked ponds and nursemaids pushed high-wheeled prams. More and more poured out of Friedrichstrasse Station and the Zoological Gardens Station, their platforms jammed as crowds flooded out of the trains. The four million figures moved down Unter den Linden and Friedrichstrasse, across Potsdamer Platz and the Tiergarten; scurrying across vast squares under umbrellas as the rain streamed down; scuttling into shop doorways beneath striped awnings bearing Gothic script; hurrying past huge department stores (Wertheim, Tietz, Karstadt-Haus, KDW); past cylindrical advertising columns, and newspaper stands; rushing down wet flights of stone steps into the passages of the underground.

The women wore coats which reached to the middle of their calves, turban-like hats, seamed stockings, and thick fox furs round their necks. The employed men wore dark double-breasted suits with turn-ups, and no man was bare-headed: they all wore hats, with rims and dark bands. The thousands of unemployed men wore collarless shirts, and caps with large peaks, and moved restlessly amongst the crowds, gathering on street-corners, or sat with bowed heads around the edges of the bowls of the fountains. Their backs were turned on the naked marble figures at the centre of the basin, where the waters from the fountain trickled down into the cold marble. All the men were in an identical posture, their faces hidden, heads down and backs bowed, their elbows resting on their knees, and the palms of their hands pressed against their ears, staring down at the ground between their feet, looking as if they were shutting out the sounds and sights of everything around them, as if, by not noticing their surroundings, they would not be noticed themselves. Bent over, alone amidst others all the same, the bowed figures concentrated on the rain-darkened ground between their feet, their hands pressed against the sides of their heads as if shutting out some tremendous sound. Long queues stretched outside the shops, cinemas, and theatres.

Cars were square and sharp-edged, had running-boards, immense mudguards, their large headlamps prominent on either side of heavy radiator grilles. They were soft-topped and open-topped, and had spare wheels in the centre of their boots, seemingly too large, and out of proportion. They pushed slowly through the crowds. Motorcycles had side-cars, and bicycles were everywhere. Buses with out-side stairs and single-decked trolley-cars moved jerkily between the pedestrians. There were many horses in the streets, and heavy cart-horses drew long carts laden with logs of wood and barrels of beer.

All over the city, thousands of children sat in rigid rows in dark heavy-wood desks, the sort with the seat attached and an ink-well inset in the top right-hand corner. The windows were high and narrow, above eye-level, and the walls beneath the windows were tiled in browns, creams, and dark greens. White chalk curled in neat Gothic script across the blackboards. The dusty light-shades were at the end of long cords suspended from high ceilings. The children repeated their nine-times table, phrases from foreign languages, irregular verbs, the dates of wars and battles in which their country had been victorious. Their words echoed in the gloomy interiors. The pens had rusty metal nibs and had to be dipped into the ink-wells after every half-sentence. In every school the hands moved backwards and forwards between the ink-wells and the paper, the hands rose into the air to answer questions, the mouths opened and closed in unison.

Young men and women in knee-length shorts, carrying tall sticks, strode up hills beneath dark fir-trees. Crowds sprawled along the shores of lakes white with the sails of boats, huddled beneath striped umbrellas, eating, sleeping, lying with eyes closed, waiting for the sun. Actresses stood at the tops of steps outside aeroplanes and waved. The planes had propellers and wicker furniture. Pilots had goggles and white silk scarves around their necks. Ciga-rettes dangled carelessly from the corners of their mouths. Zeppelins slid silently across the skies, half-lost in low clouds, and the crowds in the parks and beside the lakes looked up and pointed. Vast throngs rotated listlessly in cavernous dance-halls. People fought, outside, in the darkness, in the crowded streets, in the parks, and violence erupted at any time, murders sensational and squalid. Everywhere, there were crippled men with missing arms and legs, supporting themselves on crutches, or pushing themselves along on cut-down perambulators or little wheeled carts, past the middle-aged prostitutes leaning in groups against the walls, smoking and laughing, their faces thick with make-up.

In hundreds of cheap night-clubs, smelling of stale beer, gloomy with cigarette smoke, down dark stairs from street-level, a young woman wearing a top hat lounged back on a barrel, leaning to the left. Her right leg, nearer the audience, was drawn up until its heel rested against the knee of her left leg. Her hands were clasped around the raised knee. She was wearing high heels, dark stockings, and a suspender belt, and her short skirt was bunched up around her thighs, her frilled knickers exposed. The expression on her face was mocking, amused, sardonic. Middle-aged men watched her, rapt, awed, aroused, as she lay back sneering at them. Thin undernourished girls posed naked in shaky tableaux on tiny stages, the beams of the floodlights cloudy with the dust rising from the bare boards beneath their dirty feet, their bodies shiny with sweat, dark hair sprouting in clumps from their armpits as they raised their arms. Young men dressed as carefully made-up young women, in filmy billowing dresses, struck poses of immense hauteur, their heads arched back, their profiles sharp, believing themselves to look glamorous and desirable, as they preened, and kissed each other. They were too tall, and their hands were too large, though they painstakingly shaved their jaws and legs.

In dark cluttered rooms all over the city, in the enormous wastelands of tall tenements, the crowded acres behind the public buildings, children, boys and girls with pale and tired faces, lay on unmade beds with dirty sheets, pushed into corners, as foreigners who could not speak German undressed them and fondled their bodies. They did exactly all that they were told to do. Their faces had the worn, joyless look of people who were hungry and needed money.

In scores of cinemas, vast crowds sat in smoky darkness and watched impassively as, all across the city, the same images recurred in intensely contrasted black and white in all the films, full of dark shadows, claustrophobic and intensely enclosed, themes of madness and monsters, unimaginable horrors lying just behind the surface of everyday life. A terrifying figure with long hanging fingers and hypnotic eyes lurched across the angled roofs of a stylised city. A city lay deep beneath the surface of the earth, the mindless corridors of an oppressive city of the future, crowded with thousands of dehumanised people moving as one, the buried, submerged workers. A web of electricity created a powerful robot which looked like a beautiful woman. Floods poured through underground passages towards forgotten children. Hands clutched and gesticulated. A monster, made of clay, was brought to life to save a persecuted people. A murderer of children, tracked down through the crowded streets of a great city, his face avid and tortured, was unable to explain what made him do what he had to do as he moved towards a little girl, who looked up, smiling, towards the unseen killer, his shadow thrown across a poster behind her, seeking help to trap a murderer. A master criminal held the power of life and death over people who had not even heard of him as he worked to dominate the world secretly, altering and deciding the lives of millions. The director of an asylum, controlled by his patients, was hypnotised by a madman. Dancers moved in geometric patterns, absolutely in step, their bodies a tiny part of a larger design.

Audiences sat and watched as the flickering light from

the screens played on their faces in the smoky halls, now in darkness, now in light.

An image of a man filled the whole screen. The camera looked up at him from below, so that he seemed larger than life, towering upwards like a statue in a temple to which crowds brought worship and sacrifice. His right arm was raised, rigid, and away from his body, so that the arm, the light behind it, was a dark and solid diagonal across the screen from the top left to the centre. His left hand clasped the heavy square buckle on the thick leather belt around his waist. The knuckles were pronounced in the heavy shadowing of the black-and-white image. A belt ran diagonally across his chest from his right shoulder, paralleling the dark line of the right arm. Pockets with buttoned flaps were on either side of this belt, to the right and left of his chest, the right pocket slightly raised and puckered by the raising of the arm. His tie, with a tiny knot, was slightly awry. His eyes were in heavy darkness, and the dark moustache, with the shadow from his nose, blotted out the area from the nostrils to below the top lip, like dark blood from a bleeding nose. His neck was in deep shadow, and his ears protruded. He leaned back slightly to accommodate the balance of his body against the raised arm. He was posed against the sky, and clouds moved behind him as he stood there, exalted, godlike, carefully posed in this startlingly histrionic position, assuming an expression of stern resolve. Stirring music played, and he stood there, amid the clouds, greater than life, his shadow immense, his power absolute, his confidence unshakeable, staring into a future which would be of his creation. Nothing else mattered but this.

In front of him, perfectly in line, was a huge contingent of men in black breeches, stripped to the waist. Their stance was relaxed, their legs at ease, slightly apart, and they were holding spades, their hands resting on the han-

dle at waist height, the bright metal cutting edge touching
on the ground between their feet. At first, with their naked
chests and black breeches, they looked like medieval
headsmen holding their axes, all the executioners of history gathered together in one place.

Outside the cinema, the crowds moved up and down the
streets of the nation which was a city called Berlin.

The people moved quickly, rather jerkily, slightly
blurred, in a grainy scratched atmosphere of black and
white, or a smeary sepia, as though everything were discoloured with rolling banks of smoke. The synchronisa-
tion was not quite right, and the people seemed to rush
headlong down the streets. A voice commented on their
actions, rather heavily jocular, or theatrically serious, with
a liking for alliteration, stressing every fourth word. The
voice spoke English, and was totally devoid of all genuine
emotion, as though the people did not matter, were already lost in history. The words were quite separate from
the scenes they purported to describe.

A little boy called Emil—wearing the dark blue Sunday
suit that his mother cleaned by holding him between her
knees and scrubbing with a dampened clothes-brush, and
who wanted him to go to a good school—pushed his way
through the crowds, holding a suitcase and a bunch of
flowers for his aunt. He was followed by a crowd of children. He was searching for a thief who had stolen the
money that was intended for his grandmother.

Everyone was gazing into the distance, in silence. Children were carried on their father's shoulders, held by the
ankles, gazing into the distance, along with their parents.
The people had strong faces, rosy, tanned by the sun in
past years, and hands were held up over eyes screwed up
against the falling rain. The reflections of the buildings
and the crowds were very distinct on the soaked streets.
Their right arms were lifted into the air, at an angle up

and away from their bodies, pushing forward against each other, like children keen to answer questions in class, thrusting up their hands—"Please, sir! Please, sir!"—all those enthusiastic children, desperate for the approval of their watching teacher, who paused, looking out over the class, noticing those who did not know the answer.

The crowds, stretching far away into the distance, wandering aimlessly year after year, had found someone to give their wandering a purpose, to shape them into a pattern, to make all the millions of them a part of history. Their lives did not belong to them any more. Each individual had ceased to exist. The city, crowded with millions of people, had become a dot on a map.

H E   S A W a long line of people stretching away into the distance.

He saw women in calf-length grey overcoats, long dark hair, stumbling forward holding their children's hands, families trying to cling together, men in dark clothes, heads bowed, carrying suitcases, a long procession trudging through the snow, unarmed, surrendering. They did not cry, or call for help, but stared with eyes full of all that they had seen. Their eyes were the only part of them he could see. He could never see them clearly. They were always partially hidden by the falling snow, and the barbed wire which surrounded them. As they moved forward, the snow began to fill in their footsteps. Long, sealed trains travelled eastward, through the snow, to unknown destinations, unknown places with strange names, a foreign country a long way from home, an immense and frozen emptiness.

Their names were not known, and everything about them was forgotten. They would die, just like all the others, he thought, without names, without faces.

8

HE WAS at the beginning of a story of which he already knew the ending.

In fairy-tales collected by the Brothers Grimm, the innocent and the pure in heart always seemed to triumph, even after much fear and suffering: Hansel and Gretel outwitted the witch and escaped; the seven little kids and their mother destroyed the wolf; the three sisters in "Fitcher's Bird" overpowered even death itself to defeat the murdering magician. But he could still remember the mounting desolation with which he read some of the Hans Christian Andersen fairy-tales when he was little. He had read them over and over again, hoping that this time the ending would be a happy ending, but the endings never changed: the little match-girl died entirely alone, frozen to death on New Year's Eve, surrounded by burned-out matches; the little mermaid melted into foam after bearing her suffering bravely; and the steadfast tin soldier and the ballerina perished in the flames of the stove, leaving only a little tin heart and a metal sequin behind. He had been unable to put them away and forget about them. He had been drawn, compulsively, to read them with engrossed attention, and had wept as he found himself realising what the inevitable and unchanged end of the story would be.

IT WAS raining again outside, and the wind blew in strong gusts. The sea was only a slightly darker grey than the sky, dull, reflectionless, possessed of great depths. The curtainless windows rattled and swam, and the empty playing-fields were drab and distorted. Low black clouds rolled heavily across the sky, like smoke from a burning city.

In the 1930s, though the school, then as now, had been a boys' school, the Ferry House had been turned into a house for a small number of refugee German girls, sisters of boys in the school, or girls on their own, and the school's youngest boys, who had previously slept there, had been transferred to the main building. He had learned this from the letters, never having known it before.

He looked around the bare white walls of the echoing, bare-boarded bedroom, and thought of Lotte Goetzel, Hedwig Grünbaum, Anna Kahn, Stefanie Peters, and all the other little girls, lying in bed, pictures and postcards on the walls, listening to rain falling, and thinking of their families in Berlin, writing the letters that he was now holding in his hands.

In July, 1938, Lotte Goetzel had rejoined her parents in Berlin, after being at Southwold for two terms, and had not returned to the school.

> *Berlin-Charlottenburg 2*
> 9th August 1938

Dear Mr. High,

Growing difficulties make it impossible for us to send our daughter back to Southwold. We have now lost all our business and it is impossible for us to pay the fees any longer. We know no one who can help us. Lotte was very glad to see her family, friends, and her little dog here, but we know she will miss the kindness she was shown in

England. She was very unhappy in a strange land sometimes, but we know how much you tried to make her feel
"at home." We think it, perhaps, was too early to separate
the child from home. As she is such a shy, quiet girl, we
were really afraid that she felt so homesick so far away
from us. You may think this is sentimental in us, but I
think, as a father, you will understand our feelings. It
would be our wish to give her in your school if we could,
but perhaps it was too early. She is only 12.

We are leaving Germany, and going to Holland. I have
good hope of a position with a firm in Amsterdam. There
is a Jewish school for children from Germany, and we
hope to give Lotte a practical education so that she may be
able to earn her own money by her hands, wherever she
goes, with what the future may bring for us. All our
furniture is packed and waiting to be sent away, but we do
not know whether it will be possible to take it with us.

We thank you with all our hearts for all you have done
for Lotte. She sends a letter for you.

With many good wishes for you and your school,

Peter and Aline Goetzel

Dear Mr. High,

I am so sorry that I did not say goodbye properly to you
and Misses High. I was too unsure. Thank you for the
nice report.

The sea was rough when we crossed, and most of the
passengers were sick. Hanno Weiler and I were not.
Hanno looked after me very nicely. His mother and
father kindly took me home from Hamburg, on their way
back.

I am now hier in our house, and it is going to be sold.
It was very exciting to help to get everything ready, and
empty all the cupboards. A lot of lovely old things we
found, where we never knew from. It was great fun.

Grossvater is going to sell his farm and come with us to
Holland. It is a big adventure.

Mutti and Vati like the school foto very much. Vati
has put it under glass, and all my friends like it.

Love to you and Misses High,

Your affectionate pupil,

Lotte Goetzel

I send you a foto. Please keep me in good memory.

The little dark-haired girl stood at the edge of an empty
field, holding a small Scotch terrier, smiling up at the camera. She wore a headband in her short hair, and was wearing a pinafore dress, with a brooch in the shape of a
swan.

In October a postcard had come from the Goetzels saying that they were safe in Amsterdam, and that was the
last communication the family made with the school.

Anne Frank and her family had been German refugees
in Amsterdam.

Some years ago, when they had been in the Netherlands
(Jo had been seven, and had told all his friends at school
that they were going to Never Never Land), they had
visited the Anne Frank house in Amsterdam, where the
secret hide-out of the Frank family and their friends was
preserved, where they had hidden for two years before
being found and sent to Auschwitz and Bergen-Belsen.
Corrie had a blurred memory of darkness, and echoing
bareness, and, above all else, a little section of the wall
where the remains of some pictures and postcards stuck
there by Anne Frank had been preserved. The memory he
retained more than any other was a postcard of Princess
Elizabeth and Princess Margaret Rose. That single postcard had brought the dead girl very close to him. On
another wall were pencil lines where the parents had
marked the heights of their children as they grew towards

adulthood, month by month; and a map where pins showed the advance of the allies through northern France, nearer and nearer with every week that passed.

In spite of everything, she had written, less than three weeks before she and her family were taken away—his father had talked about the visit to the Anne Frank house in a school assembly, before he became headmaster, and read from her diary—*I still believe that people are really good at heart. I simply can't build up my hopes on a foundation consisting of confusion, misery, and death. I see the world gradually being turned into a wilderness. I hear the ever-approaching thunder, which will destroy us too. I can feel the sufferings of millions and yet, if I look up into the heavens, I think that it will all come right, that this cruelty too will end, and that peace and tranquillity will return again.*

On television, a few weeks ago, a Dutch woman journalist, a sympathiser with Red Phoenix, had been interviewed about her comments on the current trials of terrorists in West Germany (the same terrorists, now imprisoned, for whom Red Phoenix were holding the Berlin schoolchildren hostage), and the interviewer had mentioned Anne Frank's name in response to a remark about the Palestine Liberation Organisation. The woman had laughed, not sarcastically or ironically, but with genuine amusement, and called the diary her "least favourite work of fiction." "This figure of six million dead Jews," she had said, "must have been chosen, I suppose, for some cabbalistic significance, and everyone knows it has little basis in factual accuracy. It is a hoax. Surely you have read the books that prove this? It is a fiction sustained by Zionist propaganda to attempt to give some historical justification for the acts of Jewish military aggression against the Palestinian people. Some Jews did die in the war, of course, but so did millions of Poles and Russian civilians—and the figures here are not open to question. People always die in war." The programme had ended with her laughing face, amused and incredulous at the interviewer's naïvety, like a bright young lawyer defending a war criminal. When the film of *The Diary of Anne Frank* had been shown on television, all the characters speaking with American accents, a boy in Jo's class had written: "It was in black and white. It was about a girl who was hidden from the Germans in a small room, and she wrote a diary about it, but at the end the Germans found her and her friends. It was a long film, but there wasn't any fighting in it. It was set in the nineteenth century."

Always, as he worked through the confused and decimated contents of the files, through 1933, 1934, 1935, 1936, he had been aware of 1939 ahead of him, and of what was to happen in the years that followed. He knew that when one day in 1939 was reached, a door would close forever on these people, and they would never be heard of again.

There were fragments, as he moved—like an archaeologist piecing together the broken bits of bone or pottery in a destroyed and long-forgotten city—through the final files of 1939, badly burned many years previously, the remains of photographs, postcards, and letters, blackened and charred at the edges, falling into ash, crumbling away like documents in a tomb exposed to the light of day: the final letters of those people in Berlin, Leonie Matthias, Nickolaus Mittler, Mrs. Viehmann, and all the others, as the doors closed, one by one.

MRS. VIEHMANN, the mother of Kurt and Thomas, was one of the parents he had come to know best.

The last letter he had found from her had been posted

on the twenty-seventh of June, 1939. It had no address, was typed—all her other letters had been handwritten—and was unsigned. In pencil, Mr. High's secretary had written "Mrs. Viehmann" at the top.

Dear Mr. High,

I am ashamed that it is so very long a time, and we have not written to you, and we wished to do it long ago, but you must certainly know what horrible things have happened here in the time since. I have not told you, but my husband is imprisoned since the 10th November. You will, I think, know the events of that time. I have not told my children, and beg you not to tell them, because they will be so frightened and anxious, that they will not be able to learn anything at school, and it would be of no use to concern them, because they can do nothing at all to help us, as, it seems, I cannot myself. I now type all my letters, and write to both my children in the names of myself and my husband, and so they do not realise what has happened to their father. I want, also, so awfully much the money for the posting. I would be grateful if you could excuse me, that I beg you to give the letter enclosed to my sons.

I would be very happy if you should have the kindness to write to me, and tell me what you think about my children, and how they progress, especially Kurt and his future, as soon he will leave the school. Although we have to live now for the day alone, my husband and I cannot help thinking sometimes of the future. Our children now, even more than before, are all our future, and all that happens there. I have not the hope that we shall be able soon to discuss the matter of Kurt's career with you in England, because even if my husband is free from the prison, and receives a permit for England, then we have

to wait for our papers here in Berlin. That will last many
months, and we hear so from our friends who try. I have
already a permit for domestic work in England, and I do
all things possible to deliver my dear husband, but events
are stronger than I am.

Kurt, I think, wishes to be a surgeon, but do you think
this is possible that he can be educated to a profession,
without the money? Rudolf, I know, had to leave school
early and begin work of a practical kind, because of the
times in which we live. Many years are needed for study.
We feel great sorrow that we cannot care for our sons as
we would like to do, and must be obliged to ask for the
help of friends so many miles away. (Help, dear Mr. High,
that has been so willingly given to us.) We would be
grateful for your advice in this matter. Kurt may have to
go to America later, but it may last years since he must
wait until his turn.

Thank you for telling me when Thomas was ill. I beg
you, when the boy is ill, please continue to let me know.
Do not be too careful of me. I am more quiet when I
know. Thomas is still, I think, unhappy in his heart,
although he does not say so in his letters. Please forgive
him and understand him, Mr. High. He is young, but he
has known much, the torture of the last years and the
separation from his home and his family, the things which
hurt us who are grown-up, and even more a child. He has
a great need for affection which we gave him with all our
hearts when we were with him, and could hold him in
our arms. If the noisy and lively surroundings of the other
boys, as is usual and natural in a school, seem to make him
sad, it is because our house was always quiet, and my son,
after all this time, must still remember this. For me, as a
mother, it is difficult to ask you to do what I should do
myself, but please, Mr. High, could you speak kindly to

our son so that he may become more cheerful inside? I
hope you will be pleased with him. Your last observation
in his school report, and the school photograph, filled our
hearts with the utmost joy. Our sons are very well-looking,
both, and seem so tall.

Thank you for all the good things you do for our boys.

All is incertain, but we look forward impatiently to
the chance to come to England, and be with our boys
again. We have still hope that the police will return our
passports. I hope you and Misses High are in good health.

Excuse me, for troubling you so much.

> Affectionately yours,
> The mother of the boys
> you called "gifted"

THROUGHOUT July and August, the postcards from
Nickolaus Mittler had arrived at the school. Every week,
there was a new one, carefully and neatly written, each
view on the front chosen to be different.

> *Berlin-Charlottenburg*
> 27th June 1939

Dear Mr. High,

Would you be so very kind and write to me what is the
matter with the permits for me and my big brother to
come to England? Are the applications for the permit in
the home office already? I wish to give as little trouble as
possible, but I worry because my parents have the permission to come to England, and they wait only for the
permits for us.

> Yours respectfully,
> Nickolaus Mittler

Berlin-Charlottenburg
3rd July 1939

Dear Mr. High,

Could you please send me a certificate, stating that you are admitting me and my big brother to your school? The authorities here in Berlin state that we must produce this document to show that we are really going to come to your school, and then they will allow us to have passports. This document must be authenticated in England. Please send this to me signed by the authorised department. Do you need any other documents? We have our photographs, and doctor's certificates.

Yours respectfully,
Nickolaus Mittler

Berlin-Charlottenburg
9th July 1939

Dear Mr. High,

Thank you so much for kindly sending me the certificate. The Berlin passport office now says that the certificate must be made out in German, not in English. The passport office also says that your signature must be authenticated by the police of your district. Thank you so much for your trouble. I am sorry to be a nuisance. When we have the permits we will need to wait more weeks before we can get the passports, but we wait hopefully. When we get the passports we will go to the British Passport Central Office for a visa. Then all will be ready to start for England.

Yours respectfully,
Nickolaus Mittler

Berlin-Charlottenburg
15th July 1939

Dear Mr. High,

Please would you not be indignant if I once more am
compelled to write to you. The British Consulate here
requires a letter from you in which you confirm that me
and my big brother are to be accepted into your school.
The Consulate must know from your letter that a
guarantor has been found for the paying of the school fees
in England, and then it will grant the permission for us
to enter England. I beg you to send me this letter. What
cloathings will we need for the school?

Yours respectfully,
Nickolaus Mittler

Berlin-Charlottenburg
21st July 1939

Dear Mr. High,

Thank you very much for the letter you kindly sent me.
I took the letter to the British Consulate of our city, but
I beg to inform you that the letter did not contain the
guarantee that someone had been found to pay my fees,
and the Consulate demands this before it will give permission for us to enter England. What we need is only a
form! I shall not forget all your endeavours to help us. I
am so sorry to force your amicability so often. I shall try
to repay all you are doing when I come to England. We
have bought our cloathings ready.

Yours respectfully,
Nickolaus Mittler

AT THE end of August, 1939, Leonie Matthias, who
had written often from Berlin for the Jewish agency "Elternhilfe für die jüdische Jugend," asking for help for new

children, or making enquiries about the progress of children who had been received into the school, wrote from a
city many hundreds of miles away from Berlin. Elternhilfe
had been closed down by the German authorities on the
tenth of November, 1938, and she wrote as a welfare
worker in another children's relief organisation.

"Since the events of last November, a very large number of Jewish schoolchildren are gathered here, and we are
trying, with every means at our disposal, to ensure that
there can be some way in which their higher education
may continue. Could you possibly agree to accepting a few
more children? I would take as much trouble as I did from
Elternhilfe to ensure that the pupils I recommend to you
would fit in well with your school. Please give my best
wishes to the children I know in Southwold. Has Stefanie
Peters settled in well? I would like to hear how they are all
progressing. I had a very nice letter from Kurt Viehmann
the other week.

"I hope you do not mind if I enclose a photograph of an
eleven-year-old girl, Ruth Martin, an only child whose
parents owned a farm in Saxony. Her uncle managed to
emigrate to America, and he is trying to raise a financial
guarantee for her. Her parents hope to go to America,
also, in the near future. She is a very nice, friendly little
girl, and I am sure that she will fit in very well. She has
started to learn English, and is making good progress."

Ruth Martin's photograph had been removed from an
album. There were little patches of blue paper at each
corner where it had been pulled away from the page on
which it had been glued, and on the back someone had
written, in pencil: *Unsere Ruth an ihrem elften Geburt-
stag.*

Everywhere, in the final file, were the photographs of
children.

He found himself looking at the photographs, searching

for death in the children's faces, afraid of the feelings inside himself, trying not to think of the future, trying not to visualise what he knew was deep inside his head.

From November, 1938, onwards, the photographs, letters, and school reports had flooded into the school in greatly increased numbers as parents tried to find somewhere to send their children—far too many of them for it ever to have been possible for more than a very few of them to be offered places. The vanished children smiled in all the photographs as their parents waited for someone to decide whether they would live or die. Some photographs, like Ruth Martin's, were taken from family albums; others seemed to have been taken specially for the application, the child's eyes showing an awareness that the attractiveness of his smile was the most important thing in the world to his parents.

. . . These two little boys have all their papers in order, and could leave Berlin immediately, if there were a school available for them in England, and if someone could guarantee their payments for them. . . . Elise is ready for travelling since a long time, but she is waiting still for her permit from the "Home Office." . . . Sehr geehrter Mr. High, Frau Clara Werth gab mir Ihre werte Adresse, da ich beabsichtige, meine Söhne nach England zu geben. Die Jungen sind vor allem in Sport und Musik sehr begabt und singen sehr schön. Meine Kinder sind Halbwaisen, der Vater war Bankvorsteher. Da wir jüdisch sind. . . . Lucie is thirteen, and can draw nicely, and plays the piano very beautiful. She wishes to be a nurse and help the ill people, because she is a gentle girl who would like that everybody should have his place in the sun. Whatever I say about her, you will say that it is only the mother talking, but I will tell you something of the nature of my little girl so that you may see freely for yourself. One time I brought home Lucie from school, and at the door was a beggar

*with a child, who, I confess, I did not remark then, but
Lucie did. I talked with my friend who was waiting in the
house for me, and we was always disturbed by Lucie, who
always would try to call me aside, and anger me. I sent her
from the room, but when my friend went away, Lucie ran
back in and begged for food for the beggar. The beggar
was gone away and she returned weeping, and was not to
be moved to eat her supper. This is the kind of child she
is, and I implore that you will accept her in your school. . . .
I am told that you accept German boys in your school. I
have a grandson of fourteen. . . . Dieter ist ein ausgezeich-
neter Schüler. Er ist gewandt und mutig und beweist im
sportlichen Kampf Fairness und. . . . I am very sorry to
have to tell you that Emmy and Doro Werth were not
evacuated from Germany in time to escape the war. They
were to have come across in a children's transport in the
second week in September in time for the beginning of
term. When we realised how extreme the danger was, it
was too late to advance the date of their leaving, and all
the German trains had been reserved for the exclusive use
of troops for days before the war actually started. Walter,
I know, will have realised that his sisters have not made it
in time. . . .*

H A N D in hand, the little boy and the little girl stood at
the edge of the dark pathless forest, in which the wild
animals were waiting to tear them to pieces. The boy
looked back towards his home, but the adult gripped his
arm and pulled him away.

Corrie had seen, in school history books, some of the
photographs of what had happened within that dark forest,
facts to be learned by children for examinations now, like
the date of the Battle of Hastings, and what the Magna
Carta was. Before he moved up from the infants' school to

the junior school, he had decided that the date of the Battle of Hastings and the meaning of the Magna Carta were questions that he was bound to be asked, and he had learned them carefully, confident of impressing everyone with his erudition. On his first day at junior school, a teacher had approached him and opened her mouth. He had thought that the long-awaited moment had come, and that she was going to ask him for the date of the Battle of Hastings, but all she had asked him was his name and what class he was in. He had sat down in his place and eagerly awaited the opportunity to answer a question about the Battle of Hastings or the Magna Carta. Eight years had passed since then, and he was still waiting for someone to ask him for the date of the Battle of Hastings. But, even if no one ever did ask him, he still knew the answer.

The S.S. man stood with his sub-machine-gun, his face impassive, a man doing his job, rather bored. The little boy wearing the cloth cap, his short coat reaching to above his knees, stood with his arms in the air, as he had been told, his face frightened and bewildered. He was about six or seven years old. Women and other children were all around him, being rounded up. A woman just behind him, a young housewife in a headscarf, holding a heavy bag in her left hand, was only able to lift her right arm in surrender, a band with the Star of David around the top of her arm, like the black band of mourning that people sometimes wore after a death in the family. Beside the little boy was a woman, both hands raised, looking back at the face of the man with the sub-machine-gun, as if memorising what he looked like. She had a battered zip-up bag over each arm, like the full shopping-bags of a woman returned home to her family in the evening after taking a bus from the city centre.

It was a picture he had often studied. There were no

bodies, no blood, and only one gun was visible, but to him it was the image of war, the most horrifying photograph he knew of the Second World War. He thought of the Ingmar Bergman film his father had ordered for the Film Society, the two women alone on the lonely island, the nurse and her patient, the actress, who had retreated into total silence, studying that same photograph.

THERE was a newsagent's shop in Lowestoft where he was not known, and which he always visited on his infrequent journeys there on the bus, to go to the cinema, or just to walk around, away from Southwold. The women's magazines, and the comics for children—frames in war comics where immense German soldiers screamed in agony as flames from flame-throwers hit them full in the face, as a grinning British private shouted, "Try that for size, Fritzy!!"—were at the front of the shop, opposite the counter, covers forward on sloping stands. At the back of the shop, in the far corner, where he always went, trying to appear casual and offhand, was the section labelled "Adult Publications." Adult meant sex. Adult meant filth. Adult meant brutality and excitement. That was what being an adult meant.

He stared at the photographs in the magazines he took from the revolving stands, at the genitals of the naked young men to compare them with his own, at the naked women with their legs wide open, pinned out like Biology illustrations—clitoris, vagina—their fingers pushing down on themselves, holding themselves open like imperfectly healed wounds after an operation. They were like beggars in a distant land, the edge of a desert, thrusting mutilations into the faces of tourists, the only way they had of making money.

The same racks which held pornographic magazines

also held American magazines with crudely drawn covers of tall S.S. officers beating near-naked women with leather whips; and thick paperbacks about concentration camps and war atrocities. Fascinated but appalled, avid and disgusted, he gazed at them, unable to avert his eyes, the intensity of his gaze only equalled by the intensity of his gaze between the legs of the naked women in the photographs, their faces contorted into expressions of mock ecstasy, their tongues protruding from the corners of their mouths like women who had been strangled.

On the outside covers of the paperbacks were reviews from obscure newspapers in American cities, always ending in exclamation marks, always in block capital letters. Inside the books he found himself staring absorbedly at the photographs of what lay at the end of those long railway journeys, those many, many trains converging from all over Europe on the concentration camps, and the extermination camps, those places with clumsy, uncouth names far away in the east, in Poland: Majdanek, Treblinka, Chelmno, Sobibor, Belzec, Auschwitz. With compulsion and dread he stared at the heaped masses of skeletal bodies, long thin arms and legs like the pale twisted roots of heaped and rotting vegetables lying crushed beneath the earth, and brought to light, mouths open as if screaming, stomachs fallen away beneath the jutting ribcages, the impenetrable thicket of limbs; stared as he turned the books at different angles, trying to recognise human faces, trying to see the expressions on them, the hideous things that had once been men, women, and children.

T H E Y had names. They had faces.

He held their letters in his hand, he recognised their handwriting, he knew their names, he saw their faces, he had shared their most private hopes and fears, he knew who had not managed to leave Germany in time. He knew the obscenity that lay ahead for these families, parents and children, walking together hand in hand in that darkness, carrying their possessions in suitcases and in rucksacks from family camping holidays.

Some things were not to be thought of. Some things were not to be endured. In nearby countries, only a few years earlier, in the lifetime of his mother and father, millions of people had been humiliated, robbed, degraded, and murdered, the populations of entire cities.

If Hitler had completely succeeded, would the Jewish people have become a lost and legendary race, cloaked in mysteries and myths, like the Babylonians and the Assyrians, as distant and strange as the Old Testament people in an illustrated children's Bible? Opposite the English translation of *The Children's Haggadah*, sections of the book had been printed in Hebrew script, like the carving of forgotten alphabets on fragments of stone in museums. *This year we sit at the table half glad, half sad, here, far away from our own land; but next year we hope to welcome a joyous Seder in the land of Israel. This year we are still as unhappy as slaves in many countries, but next year we pray to be a free and happy people.*

H E H A D been sitting in the bare room for a long time.

Before he closed the door of the inner room in the bedroom, and turned the key on the returned and neatly sorted files, he looked at the photograph on the front of the final postcard from Nickolaus Mittler, the sepia faded and cold—as in all the other postcards—like a picture of something from long, long ago.

Friedrichsbrücke und Nationalgalerie, Berlin. (Friedrich Bridge and National Gallery, Berlin.)

He was looking at a scene which was like a model he had once seen in a museum, a reconstruction of Imperial Rome, stone statues dark against the skyline, naked and draped figures of gods and goddesses, columns and colonnades stretching into the distance. The bridge—the same bridge that had been visible in the distance in the aerial view of the cathedral—crossed the river in three shallow arches, with figures as tall as three-storey houses holding lamps in the shape of torches high into the sky, two on each side of the bridge, above the foundations between the arches. Four tall columns, one at each side of the approaches to the bridge, were surmounted by colossal eagles about to soar into flight. Beyond the bridge, on the far side of the river, lining its bank as far as another bridge in the distance, a row of tall columns rose straight up, like an illustration in an art book of the five orders of architecture, shafts, capitals, and architraves enclosing a columned building with a pediment, like the Acropolis or the Capitol, the great national temple, rising above its surroundings, floating above the trees, the columns, and the river. The whole scene was like a triumphal way through a pagan city, along which slaves were to be led into perpetual bondage.

Victory was everywhere in the immense city, stretching away across the plain to the forest and the mountains: on the column in front of the Reichstag, huge, winged, holding aloft a wreath for the victor in her right hand; above the Brandenburg Gate, the trees of Unter der Linden so large and close together in the boulevard that the street seemed like a long narrow park between solid walls of buildings; in the soaring eagles on the Friedrich Bridge— everywhere was victory, victory, victory.

The whole city was depopulated, all its people vanished. There had been no human figure in any of the photographs on the postcards from Nickolaus Mittler. The massive buildings, larger than any human scale, were there for ever, more solid and important than the ephemeral figures, tiny and fragile, of men, women, and children holding hands to stay together. The streets of the great deserted city stood out in sharp relief in the cold light of early morning or late winter afternoon. The columns of shadows were long, stretching away and narrowing into the distance.

The same shadows stretched out across the empty playing-fields outside the window.

Scientists had now invented a bomb which could destroy human beings but leave buildings undamaged. The body's cell structure disintegrated, the molecules came apart.

JO'S COPY of *Emil and the Detectives* was a Thomas Nelson school edition, a reprint of 1942.

The English schoolchildren in their evacuated school read about the adventures of Berlin schoolchildren as the bombs rained down on Berlin from the English planes. On the Contents list it said: "III. The Journey to Berlin Begins: 26." Corrie thought of the boys in Nollendorf Square, saying good night to each other and shaking hands like grown-up men who are very serious about something.

He had flicked the pages of the book over, and looked at the page open in front of him, the illustration on page thirty-nine of Emil's nightmare on the train: Emil running for his life past the skyscraper two hundred storeys high, pursued by the horses, and the train, and the engine-driver with the whip. "The city was so large, and Emil was so small."

He wondered whether Emil Tischbein was a Jewish name, and where the little boy from the small country town who loved his widowed mother would have been in 1942. Emil, Mrs. Tischbein, Grandmother, Pony Hütchen,

Aunt Martha, Uncle Heimbold, Gustav, the Professor, little Tuesday, Gerold, Friedrich the First, Arnold Mittler and his little brother: where would they all have been, what would have happened to them all, caught in the flames as the book burned?

BENT over in the quiet room, Nickolaus Mittler carefully and painstakingly wrote at the table near the window, filling the postcards with his best handwriting. He was absorbed like a figure in a Dutch interior, bowed over a letter or a musical instrument, his inner feelings possessing him more completely than his surroundings.

He needed more time.

He needed the future to approach more slowly.

9

"GOD WILL not forsake us," Hansel said to Gretel.
"Don't believe that we can ever be totally abandoned.
Sleep peacefully, my dear little sister."

They prayed, and then, comforted, they both went to
sleep.

Next day, when it was still dark, before the sun had
even started to rise, the woman came into the children's
bedroom, and woke them up, saying, "Come on, get up
you two! We have to go into the forest to collect some
wood for the fire."

She gave each of them a tiny piece of bread, and said,
"This is the only food that we've got left. Save it for your
dinner. If you eat it too soon, you'll have nothing at all to
eat later."

Gretel put both pieces of bread, hers and Hansel's, into
her pinafore pocket, because Hansel's pockets were filled
with the pebbles. Then the whole family began to walk
into the darkness of the forest.

When they had walked a little way, Hansel stood still,
and looked back towards where their home was. He did
this again and again as they walked further into the forest.

"What do you think you're doing?" his father asked
him. "You're holding us all up with your dawdling. What
on earth are you looking at?"

"I'm sorry, father," Hansel said. "I'm looking back at

my little white cat. He's sitting up on the roof, all by himself, looking for me. I never said goodbye to him."

"Don't be such a fool!" the woman said. "That's not your little cat. What you can see is the morning sun shining on the chimneys."

Hansel, however, had not been looking back at his cat, or at the sun shining on the chimneys, but to check that the white pebbles he had been secretly dropping from his pockets had been leaving a track that he would be able to follow back out of the forest.

When they had reached the very middle of the forest, where it was darkest, the father said, "Now, children, collect up some wood, and I'll light a little fire for you so that you won't be cold."

Hansel and Gretel worked quietly together, and piled up the pieces of wood they found until they had made a little white hill of dead wood. The father set fire to it, and when the flames were burning very high and very bright, and the shadows were flickering amongst the trees, the woman pretended to smile, and said, "Now, children, you must be tired. Lie down beside the fire where it's nice and warm, and your father and I will go into the forest and cut a good supply of wood. When we've collected enough, we'll come back for you, and then we can all go home, and sit round a lovely warm fire together."

The adults went away, and Hansel and Gretel sat together beside the fire. In the middle of the day they ate their little pieces of bread, and, as they could hear what they thought was the sound of an axe nearby, they thought that their father was working only a short distance away from them. It was not an axe, however, but a branch which their father had fastened loosely to a withered tree, tapping backwards and forwards as it was blown by the wind. As Hansel and Gretel sat there in the warmth, listening to the slow tap-tapping coming through the trees, their eyes began to feel heavier and heavier, and they fell into a deep sleep.

When they woke up again, the fire had long ago died out, and it was cold and dark, the deep night fallen all around them in the forest.

Gretel was frightened, and began to cry.

"We will never be able to find our way home," she sobbed to her brother. "We're too deep into the forest ever to find our way out."

Hansel put his arm about her shoulder and comforted her.

"Don't be frightened," he said. "Just wait a little while, until the moon has risen, and then we will be able to find our way home. I promise you."

When the full moon had risen above the trees around them, the white pebbles that Hansel had dropped behind him shone with a cool silvery light. He took his little sister by the hand, talking to her and encouraging her, and then began to follow the trail of pebbles through the forest.

All night long they walked through the forest, guided by the pebbles, and, just as day broke, they once again found themselves at their father's house. They knocked at the door, and the woman opened it. When she saw that it was Hansel and Gretel she disguised her real feelings, and said, "You've been very naughty and thoughtless! Why did you sleep for so long in the forest? Your father and I were beginning to think that you were never coming back!" The father, however, rejoiced inwardly, because it had almost broken his heart to leave them all alone in the dark forest.

A few months later, there was another great famine in the country, and the children, lying awake in bed, again heard their stepmother talking to their father.

"The only food we have left is half a loaf. When that has gone, it will be the end of us. We must get rid of the children. That is the only possible solution. We must again take them into the middle of the forest, and make sure, this time, that they can't find their way out again. It's the only way we can save ourselves."

The father was overcome with guilt and grief.

"We cannot do that," he said, angrily. "Parents should share their very last mouthful of food with their children. We cannot abandon them."

The woman would not listen to a word he said, and turned on him furiously, mocking and taunting him.

"Once you have failed to say 'No,' " she said, "you can never say 'No' again. Because you agreed the first time, you cannot fail to agree with me now."

She continued to argue with him, until he was compelled, once again, to agree with her.

Hansel waited until the adults were asleep, and, as he had done before, he got up, put on his coat, and tiptoed downstairs. He planned to collect the white pebbles again, and use them on the following day to save them, but it was impossible for him to do this. The woman had locked the door, and he was unable to get out.

He went back upstairs, and explained to Gretel what had happened.

His little sister began to cry, and Hansel tried to console her.

"God will never abandon us," he said to her. "Don't cry. Sleep peacefully. We will find a way out of the forest somehow."

The following morning they were again woken by the woman before the sun had risen, and she pulled them from their beds in the darkness.

The pieces of bread that were given to them were even tinier than those they had had the first time. As they began to make their way into the forest, Hansel, as he had done the previous time, stood still, and looked back towards their home, more and more often as they went deeper into the forest.

"You're slowing us all down, doing that," his father said. "Come on, keep up with the rest of us."

"Sorry," Hansel said. "I'm looking back at my little pet pigeon. He's sitting up on the roof, all by himself, looking for me. I never said goodbye to him."

"You're a fool!" the woman said. "That's not your little pigeon. All you can see is the morning sun shining on the chimneys."

Hansel had not been looking back at his pigeon, or at the sun shining on the chimneys. He had been crumbling his piece of bread in his pocket, and secretly dropping crumbs to leave a track that he would be able to follow back out of the forest. Little by little, he dropped all the crumbs, little white fragments on the dark earth.

The woman led the children into the very deepest part of the forest, to a place where they had never been before in their lives. Again, a huge fire was made, and again the woman pretended to smile, and said, "Now you stay here, children. When you feel tired, have a little sleep. We are going into the forest to cut wood for the fire at home. When we've finished, we'll come back to you in the evening, and take you back home with us."

The adults went away, leaving the two children sitting beside the fire. When the middle of the day came, Gretel shared her little piece of bread with Hansel, because he had scattered all his bread in the forest. Then they fell asleep, and night fell, but no one came for them.

They awoke, alone, in the deep blackness of the night in the forest.

Hansel again put his arm around his sister to comfort her, because she was afraid of the darkness.

"Don't be frightened," he said. "Remember what happened last time? Just wait, and when the moon has risen, we will be able to follow the trail of bread, and reach home safely."

They waited until the moon had risen above the trees, but there were no crumbs anywhere to guide them through the forest. Thousands of birds flew about the forest during the day, and they had eaten every piece of bread. The whole trail that Hansel had laid so carefully had disappeared.

Hansel took his little sister by the hand.

"Don't worry," he said. "I'm sure we'll soon be able to find the way out of the forest."

But they did not find it. They walked all through the night, and for the whole of the next day, until night fell again, but they were still in the depths of the dark forest, weak and dizzy from hunger, as they had been unable to find anything to eat except two or three berries growing on the ground. Exhausted and cold, unable to walk any further, they huddled together beneath a tree, and fell asleep.

The sun had already risen when they awoke the next morning, and it was now three mornings since they had left their father's house. They began their journeyings again, but seemed to find themselves travelling deeper and deeper into the darkness, across the black earth on which no grass grew. Hansel began to realise that they would soon die of hunger and exhaustion, and he was wondering what he could say to his little sister.

At midday, when the pale sun was visible in the sky above the trees, a lovely snow-white bird, bright against the dark trees, sat on a branch just above them, and sang so beautifully that they stood still and rapt, drinking in its song, as if to fill the hunger that was inside them. When it had finished singing, it spread its wings, and flew a short distance away from them, alighting on another tree. They walked towards it, hand in hand, stumbling and faint, Hansel helping Gretel, longing to hear that sweet music once again, and, as they drew near, the bird spread its wings again, flying just ahead of them, staying just in sight. All that afternoon, the two children followed the white bird through the forest, until, as night fell, they reached a little clearing, and the bird flew on to the roof of a little house in the centre of the clearing, and stayed there.

It was a lovely little steep-roofed house, standing amidst the trees in the quiet forest, in the cold clear air, surrounded by lawns and flower-beds, with soft warm light glowing out of its windows to guide them towards it in the rapidly falling darkness. As they came closer up to the house, they saw that it was built entirely of gingerbread, covered with little decorated biscuits, and that the windows were made of clear sugar, shining with a soft translucent glow. It was a dream come true.

"Look, Gretel," Hansel said, "our prayers are answered. We have found something to eat at last. I will reach up and eat a bit of the roof, and you can eat some of the window. It will taste nice and sweet."

Hansel stood up on tip-toe and broke off a little corner of the roof to see what it tasted like, and Gretel leant against the window, and pulled away a piece of the pane.

Faint with hunger, they were feasting on the house, when a soft little voice cried out from inside:

> "Nibble, nibble, gnaw,
> Who is nibbling at my little house?"

The children thought quickly, and then answered:

> "The wind, the wind,
> The heaven-born wind,"

and went on eating, not pausing for a moment. Hansel, in his hunger, tore away a great chunk of the roof, and Gretel pulled out a complete circular window-pane, sitting down and leaning against the wall to eat it.

Suddenly, the door of the house opened, and a very old lady, frail, bent-over, came out slowly, supporting herself on crutches. Hansel and Gretel, frightened and guilty, dropped what they had in their hands, and Hansel put his arms around his sister.

The old lady, however, smiled gently, and held out her arms.

"Oh, you poor, dear children," she said tenderly, "here in the forest all by yourselves. You must come in and let me look after you in my house. Here you will be safe. Here you will be cared for."

She took them both by the hand, and led them into her little house, talking to them kindly, and welcoming them. She sat them at the table in the little kitchen, beside the warm firelight, near a big tiled oven, and the smell of cooking filled the room. Then she set a meal before them: milk and pancakes, with sugar, apples, and nuts. Afterwards, she took them into the bedroom, where two pretty little beds were covered with soft white linen. Hansel and Gretel lay down to go to sleep, and thought they were in heaven.

The old lady had only pretended to be kind. She was, in reality, an evil witch who lay in wait for children, and who had built the little gingerbread house in order to lure them into her power. When she had a child under her control, she killed it, cooked it, and ate it, and that day was a feast day for her. Witches have red eyes, and cannot see far, but they have a keen sense of smell, like animals, and know when human-beings are nearby. When she realised that Hansel and Gretel were drawing near to her house, she laughed with malicious delight, and said, "I shall have them! They shall never escape from here."

Early the next morning, before the children were awake, she got up and went into their bedroom, and looked at them as they lay asleep in bed, young and unprotected, with their rosy cheeks, and warm breath, their hands flung back against their pillows.

"These two will taste good!" she thought, drooling.

She seized Hansel, sleepy and confused, in her shrivelled hands, and carried him behind the house into a little stable, and locked him into a cage made out of iron bars. Hansel screamed repeatedly for help, but there was no one there to hear him, or to come to his help. The immense dark forest stretched away on all sides, silent and unpopulated, empty of all humanity. Snow had started to fall, and the huge flakes fell silently from the grey sky, covering all the dark earth with a deep, trackless whiteness, dazzling to look at.

The old woman went back into the bedroom, and shook Gretel until she woke up.

"Where is Hansel?" Gretel asked at once, frightened to be alone. "Where is my big brother?"

The woman laughed, immensely amused.

"You're never going to see him again," she said. "Get up! Make yourself useful. Bring me some water from the well, and then you can cook something good for your brother. I have locked him in the stable behind the house, and I'm going to feed him up and make him fat. When he is all ready, I am going to eat him."

Gretel, terrified and lonely, sobbed as if her heart would break, but the old woman only laughed at her, and tormented her, and forced her to do all that she had commanded.

In the days that followed, as the snow continued to fall,

all the best food was cooked for Hansel, locked away out of sight in the stable, but Gretel got nothing to eat but the shells of crabs. As she worked, weak and exhausted, beaten and mocked by the old woman, she found a long corridor leading out of the kitchen, near the oven, lined with doors. Behind the doors were many rooms piled to the ceilings with all kinds of goods, all neatly stacked and sorted. One room was full of money, paper and coins from many different countries; another was full of jewellery, rings, brooches, necklaces, valuables of every type imaginable. There were rooms entirely filled with children's clothing, with shoes, with children's toys, underclothing, blankets, handkerchiefs, and hair cut from girls' heads.

Every morning, the woman went out to the little stable, and up to the cage.

"Hansel," she commanded, "put your finger out so that I can feel if you are getting any fatter."

Hansel, thinking desperately, stretched out a little bone through the bars of the cage towards her, and the woman, whose eyes were dim, thought that it was Hansel's finger, and was angry and astonished that he seemed to be getting no fatter.

Four weeks went by in this way, and Hansel still seemed to remain as thin as ever, so that the woman was seized with impatience, and decided that she was not prepared to wait any longer.

"Gretel!" she shouted at the little girl. "Bring me some water this instant. I've waited long enough. Tomorrow, whatever happens, I'm going to kill your brother, fat or thin, and cook him."

Almost blinded with tears, Gretel stumbled towards the well, the water falling unheeded from her eyes. She tried to remember what her brother had said to her, to comfort her, when he was there beside her, and could speak to her, and give her courage. "God will not forsake us," he had said. "Don't believe that we can ever be totally abandoned."

"Dear God, please help us," she cried in her despair. "If the wild animals in the forest had torn us to pieces, at least we would have died together. I'm so frightened of being all by myself."

"Stop that noise!" the woman sneered. "It won't do any good at all. No one can hear you, and no one will come and help you. Your brother dies tomorrow."

Early the next morning, when it was still dark, the woman made Gretel get up, light the fire, and hang up the cauldron full of water. Outside the windows, the snow was still falling.

"We will bake first," the woman said. "I've already heated the oven, and the dough is all kneaded and ready."

Gretel stood bowed over the cauldron, silent, the tears running down her cheeks.

"Come here," the woman said. "Stand in front of me."

Gretel did as she was told, too frightened to resist without her brother.

"Take off your clothes," the woman said.

Sobbing helplessly, frightened and alone, Gretel took off her shoes, her pinafore, her dress, and all her clothes, folding them neatly as she undressed, as she had been shown by her mother before she died.

When she was completely undressed, the woman took a pair of scissors and cut off all Gretel's hair, close to her skull. Gretel remained with her head bowed as her hair fell to the floor, the braids falling all in one piece, with the ribbon still in them.

"Give me that chain," the woman said.

Gretel unclasped the chain from round her neck. It had been a birthday present from Hansel, and had a little star at the end of it. She handed it to the woman.

She took Gretel over to the oven, from which the flames were already darting.

"Creep in," said the woman, "and see if it is properly heated for the bread."

"Hansel," Gretel whispered. "Hansel."

"Get in," the woman said, and Gretel, without saying another word, climbed up into the oven, and the woman shut the iron door, and fastened the bolt.

When she was sure that Gretel had been burnt to death, the woman went behind the house, and walked through the deep drifts of snow to the little stable, and walked up towards the iron cage where Hansel was imprisoned.

"Gretel?" Hansel called out when he heard someone approaching. "Is that you, little sister?"

"Your sister is dead," the woman said. "I put her into my oven, and she was burnt to death. Now it is time for you to die."

She opened the door of the cage.

"Get out," she said. "What are you crying for?"

Hansel stood shivering in the cold stable, his breath white. The whole stable was flooded with a hard bright light from the snow outside.

"Come here," the woman said. "Stand in front of me, and take off your clothes."

Shivering, in tears, Hansel fumbled with the fastenings of his clothes, folding them neatly as he took them off, as Gretel had.

When he was completely undressed, Hansel stood shivering helplessly, his hands cupped in front of him, his head bowed, his body pinched and white.

"Give me that ring," the woman said.

Hansel pulled at the ring until it came away from his finger, and handed it to the woman. His mother had given it to him on the day that Gretel was born, and told him that it was a present brought for him by his new little sister.

The woman took Hansel out of the stable, and into the deep snow.

"Walk to the house," she said.

His arms wrapped around himself, his body burning in the icy air, the flakes of snow like drops of fire, Hansel walked naked through the falling snow in the dark air. He saw the thick smoke pouring from the chimneys of the house.

"God, do not forsake me," he whispered. "Let my little sister be alive. Don't let me die."

She took Hansel over to the oven, where the flames were now high and bright.

"Get in," the woman said. Hansel stood for a moment, and saw his sister's hair lying on the kitchen floor, beside her neatly folded clothes. Then, without another word, he bent over, and climbed up into the oven, and the woman shut the iron door, and fastened the bolt.

When she was sure that Hansel was dead also, the woman went back out of the house, and to the stable. She closed the door of the iron cage, and picked up Hansel's clothes, then walked back to the house, closing the stable door behind her. The whole clearing around the house was white and trackless as the snow continued to fall.

Inside the house, she picked up Gretel's clothes and hair, and added the children's clothes to all the others in the room in the corridor. She put Gretel's chain and Hansel's ring in the room with all the other jewellery, and then walked back into the kitchen, and towards the oven, drooling with anticipation. Today was going to be a feast day.

She is living there still, happy and contented, living in perfect comfort and prosperity, waiting for the children who come through the forest.

10

HE TURNED at the top of the steps and stood looking back the way he had come, towards the Ferry House, out into the darkness of the playing-fields, from the terrace that ran along the back of the school buildings, above flood-level. As he looked, for a long time, out across the low-lying fields towards Dunwich, down the coast, he felt, in the darkness and cold air, as if he were at the edge of the earth, facing out across the unknown, at unmapped and desolate regions stretching endlessly away, the sound of the sea on his left. He had felt the same feeling when he was little, when he stood outside the front of the Ferry House, beyond the school grounds, and looked across the common, rising beyond the footpath, filling all the distance to the sky. It had seemed to him like the beginnings of the outside world, a mysterious and untracked wilderness where the sun went down and strange creatures lurked in the bushes and long grass.

He turned and walked towards the school, the unlighted mass of the buildings a darker solid shape against the sky. He was not a boarder in the school, and only saw the dormitories during the holidays. In his imagination, they were always empty and echoing, the beds stripped, the walls bare.

Instead of walking along the terrace to make his way out on to Dunwich Green, near Tennyson's, he went inside, switching his torch on as he opened the nearest door,

and began to walk parallel to the terrace, through the
centre of the buildings. The reflection of his own light
moved towards him, caught in the glass of class-room
doors. In the school theatre the set was still up for *The
Winter's Tale*, the tall leafless tree in the centre, its
branches spreading over the bare stage, and there was one
of the programmes designed for them by Lilli still lying on
the floor, a dusty footprint across its front cover.

His feet echoing, he passed empty class-rooms, with
writing still on the blackboards, possessions stacked neatly
in the lockers, all the children gone. The room he eventually went into was the German room, where he had hardly
ever been before, as he did not take German. He switched
on the light and sat at a desk near the door, at the back of
the room.

Above the blackboard were tables of the definite and
indefinite articles, irregular verbs, personal pronouns.
Lotte Goetzel's father had written that Lotte felt very
strange when she had heard English parents calling their
children "you," because she thought that was really a
plural pronoun, and it sounded so formal and distant. The
days of the week, and the months of the year, written in
German, which lined the walls near the ceiling, reminded
him of the letters of the alphabet which ran around the
walls in his infants' school, when there had been so much
to learn, so many tasks to master, in order to become
grown-up, a big boy: weeing like a big boy, and climbing
stairs properly, having a proper big boy's bed, tying a tie,
fastening shoe-laces. Every child, through all the years of
childhood, worked with great intentness to acquire the
skills of a proper adult person.

On the blackboard was a partially erased drawing of a
human figure, a clownish matchstick giant drawn by a
small child, the parts of the body carefully labelled: *das
Auge, der Mund, das Ohr, die Nase*; and he saw that every

object in the room had a neat little label on it, naming
what it was, as if giving that object reality, like pages in an
illustrated A.B.C.—*der Stuhl, der Tisch, die Decke, die
Tür, das Fenster*. When he had been teaching Lilli, over a
year ago, he had drawn blank maps of parts of Southwold,
and simplified sketch outlines of some of her illustrations,
asking her to write in the names of as many of the buildings or objects as she could. He remembered her clutching
her pencil fiercely, her eyes determined.

The vocabulary list pinned to the wall beside the blackboard was for *die Stadt: the town*, and the first words in
the list which followed—*die Hauptstrasse: the main
street, die Strasse: the street, die Gasse: the lane*—
reminded him of the nursery rhyme on one of the birthday
cards from Jo. *(This is the key of the kingdom: In that
kingdom is a city, In that city is a town, In that town there
is a street, In that street there winds a lane....)*

Jo had bought two cards for him, one for a ten-year-old
and one for a six-year-old, and he had found them suspended from the ceiling above his bed when he had woken
up that morning, together with a poster—"HAPPY
BIRTHDAY, BIG 16-YEAR-OLD-TYPE CORRIE"—that he had
drawn using his set of Winsor & Newton coloured inks
that had been one of Lilli's Christmas presents to him. He
loved the decorative boxes that the bottles of ink came in.
The one he liked best was the design for ultramarine ink,
where a little boy in a sailor suit knelt on a rock at the
edge of the sea, sailing a model yacht. It was like the
design on the painted enamel egg in the kitchen. Each of
the cards had Jo's signature inside, and a pencilled scrawl
that was Matthias's signature when Jo held his hand. All
that it said inside the card for the ten-year-old was *I can
do anything, now that I'm ten*. A lot of people had sent
him cards, and there had been two greetings telegrams,
one from Dad—"SIXTEEN! DON'T BULLY YOUR FRAIL

OLD DAD. MISSING YOU, SON"—and one from Cato—
"CONGRATULATIONS ON SIXTEENTH BIRTHDAY. PLAIN
BROWN PACKAGE FOLLOWS." He remembered how much
he had looked forward to his tenth birthday because his
age would be in double figures.

As a small child, he hated having his birthday so close
to Christmas. It seemed so unfair to have two such special
days so close together, reducing the time he could spend
on speculation and building up excitement, though his
parents had always been meticulous in keeping the two
occasions separate, giving his birthday an importance not
overshadowed by Christmas. He remembered asking his
mother why she hadn't chosen him on a better day. He
had hankered after the twenty-eighth of October at one
time, as something to look forward to in the middle of the
longest term of the school year. Birthdays belonged to dark
nights and cold weather: the games inside could be more
exciting then, he had thought.

W H E N he walked through into the sun lounge from Lilli's kitchen, she was on the far side, bent over her loom.
He had heard the click-click as he approached.

She moved along the bench as he came in, and he sat
beside her.

They sat in silence together as they often did for a while
before he went to bed. He leaned forward, watching the
pattern emerge, thread by thread. He looked carefully at
the design of the shawl she was making. Lilli's hands
moved smoothly backwards and forwards, up and down,
the hand nearest to him passing the shuttle swiftly away
from him.

As he had requested, there had been no formal celebration for his birthday: Lilli baked a cake, Sal came round,
there had been presents, but that was all. He would open

his presents at supper-time, the last thing before he went to bed. It was a tradition he had started when he was little, to keep his birthday presents as far away as possible from his Christmas presents. After Matthias had gone to bed, they had played Dungeons and Dragons for a time, though Sal left before the game was completed.

"Twenty questions," Corrie said.

" 'Try to speak. Try to answer without writing anything down,' " Lilli quoted to him.

"What is your name?"

"What is the name of my school?"

"What is the weather like today?"

"What season is it?"

"How old am I?"

"What part did Jo play in *The Winter's Tale*?"

"Which room are we in?"

"Don't ask me what your father's job is, will you?" Lilli asked eventually, when the questions started to become more and more bizarre.

He had been reminding Lilli of some of his early lessons with her, when he had completed his hour by firing twenty questions, trying to get her to answer automatically without the agonies of thought, insisting on complete sentences. He used to hold on gently to her hands, not allowing her to move them, so that she could make no gesture, no movement to convey words she could not utter or recall. She had been unable to think of the word for "headmaster," and although he had included the same question over and over again, she could summon up no other word for Dad's job than "big teacher" for several weeks.

"You were a very hard teacher," Lilli said, smiling.

"Inevitably, with such a troublesome pupil." Corrie assumed his most schoolmasterly voice. "I had to complain to the big teacher."

He remembered how, in his early lessons, he was self-conscious, not fully at ease, and sometimes found it difficult to talk beyond the words he had prepared for the lessons with her. He used an awkward jocularity, copied from some of his teachers, who were unsure of how to communicate with him. Now he was the teacher, and all his experience up to that time had been of being taught.

They sat together in silence again.

He remembered how the skin of Lilli's hands felt loose, as if flesh and bone beneath were too small for it, like something soft and yielding to lie against if you were tired.

"You look very thoughtful," Lilli said, some time later.

It was the usual invitation to talk.

"Not really."

"Yes, really. You've been the same all week, Corrie. Worried about the onset of old age?"

"It's just some music I'm trying to . . ."

"Yes. You have been practising a lot recently."

There was a faintly interrogative note in Lilli's comment.

He couldn't tell Lilli what his main thoughts were about, that inner room in the bedroom, that entry into the forest, pathless, grassless, black as perpetual night within a few feet of the edge.

"Jo's very unhappy at the moment, Corrie. I think he's been lonely, and wanting to talk to you. He says you've been locking yourself in the Ferry House, and staying there all day." Lilli paused. "And he hasn't heard any music from inside."

"I've been thinking."

"He was crying last night. It's the end of the year. The time when you look back."

"Mum?"

"Yes."

"He was very quiet when Sal was here."

Corrie thought for a moment.

"You're right about the end of the year. I don't feel that time has passed just because I've had my birthday today, but on New Year's Eve I'll be thinking of a whole year that's gone."

"He's missing her very badly just now. Christmas, and your father being away."

"Jo put his present in the middle of his room, so it'll be the first thing he sees when he gets back."

They had bought Dad a piece of Staffordshire pottery when Sal had taken them into Norwich, a ship called *The Three Brothers*.

"He's been upset about that school, and the terrorists as well."

That afternoon, the terrorists had set a deadline. They were going to shoot one child every half-hour, beginning at ten-fifteen, English time, that evening, and continue until they got what they wanted. Lilli had listened to the radio with the two of them to the serious, impassioned voices speaking in German, and then the reporter in Berlin translating what was being said, the telephone line crackling, breathing and heartbeats magnified by the recording. The news-reader's calm, steady voice mentioned that there was some movement of army units in the area around the school, and then went on to other items of news: the murder of a kidnap victim in Turin, an explosion in a Paris shopping-centre, the trial of an Arab gunman in London. Corrie thought of the young woman reading the evening news on the television, carefully made-up, cool, distant, like the voice of a teacher in a lecture theatre—a remote figure—speaking unemotionally of the events of an equally remote past.

"It's a quarter to ten. Let's have supper soon."

"I'll go and get Jo."

"Will you talk to him, Corrie? Brothers should help each other."

He nodded.

THERE seemed to be no one in Tennyson's when he walked through. Baskerville stood up as he went into their part of the sun lounge, to investigate who was there, peering closely at him before he went back to his basket, wagging his tail and looking vaguely gratified after Corrie scratched his head for him.

As he drew the curtains, he looked out across the Green. The lights around the horse-chestnut tree were switched on, swaying in the wind. Two boys were riding bicycles round the tree, their backs to their handlebars, facing out across the saddles, moving their feet round and round backwards, skidding on the wet grass.

He picked up a book lying on the back of the chesterfield and began to look at the illustrations. He could hear music from Jo's bedroom upstairs. Pooh and Piglet walked through the snow together. Pooh and Tigger sat at a table eating honey. Piglet planted a haycorn. Eeyore, with immense dignity, floated out from under the bridge during the game of Poohsticks. Jo had once written an essay in which he had called Eeyore his favourite character in fiction.

He looked at the picture of Piglet's ears streaming behind him like banners, and then walked out into the hall to call upstairs.

"Jo?"

He started up the stairs in the darkness.

"Jo?"

The words from the *Saint Matthew Passion* filled the staircase, the whole of the quiet house. The voice soared.

> *"Erbarme dich, mein Gott,*
> *Um meiner Zähren willen;*
> *Schaue hier, Herz und Auge*
> *Weint vor dir bitterlich.*
> *Erbarme dich!"*

It was an aria which always filled him with emotion and made him feel close to tears, like the moment in *Le Grand Meaulnes* when Meaulnes clutched his baby daughter in his arms, sobbing at the death of his young wife, or the moment in *Romeo and Juliet* when Juliet kissed the dead Romeo and cried, "Thy lips are warm." He was tender-hearted, easily moved. He had fought to control his tears when the Film Society had shown those two films, been unable to speak afterwards, moved by the death of children.

There was no one in Jo's bedroom.

His boots and his socks were lying beside the bed, and the T-shirt he had been wearing that day: "My parents went to Bermuda, and all they brought back for me was this lousy T-shirt."

He looked at the Advent calendar from one of Jo's old ladies.

It was a picture of a city in the east. Kings with gifts were riding towards it. Flat-topped roofs and battlemented towers rose into the night sky. A bright star was shining, a light to illuminate the whole of the city and its crowded streets, long ago. Tree-covered hills rose to the distant dark mass of mountains, beyond a lake whose deserted shore was lined with fishing-boats. Every morning from the first of December, Matthias had come into Jo's room very early to open one of the twenty-four little doors in the city, to reveal the secret scene inside, to wake Jo and tell him what that day's scene was. The calendar hung in front of the light on the wall, so that Jo could see it as he lay in bed, and so that the light would glow through the scenes behind the little doors, all of them now open, revealing angels rejoicing, birds in the sky, fish in the lake, families sitting at meals together, musical instruments, cattle and donkeys in the stable. On the morning of Christmas Eve, Matthias had opened the last little door, the most elaborate and beautiful of all the pictures. In the warm candlelit interior, the young mother gazed lovingly at the baby who was born to die.

It was a German Advent calendar, printed in Munich.

> *Erbarme dich, mein Gott,*
> *Um meiner Zähren willen.*

On the eighteenth of December, Matthias woke Jo to tell him the morning's picture was of a radiator. Baffled, Jo had got out of bed to investigate, and found an illustration of a harp.

He saw wet footprints on the carpet, leading away from the record-player, and followed them through into the bathroom, putting on the light in the corridor.

Jo was sitting in the bath.

Corrie sat on the lid of the lavatory pedestal, and leaned back, stretching his legs out.

"I shall avert my eyes if my presence is inhibiting your performance," Jo said. He had a very crisp, clear voice. He was frequently told he spoke "very good English."

The room was in darkness, and Jo's skin looked very white, gleaming faintly in the light that shone through the open door from the corridor.

As Corrie watched, Jo closed his eyes, held his head very upright, and shook it rapidly from side to side, a gesture he often made so that his hair would fall neatly into place.

He moved across and sat on the edge of the bath.

Jo was not having a bath. His chest was bare, but he was dressed in the jeans that Sal had bought him for Christmas, and sitting in the half-filled bath to shrink them to size. He was peering closely at a book. A carton of yoghurt stood in the soap-rack. The water was already a deep shade of blue.

"How long have you been in there?"

"An hour or so." He spoke very quietly, his voice expressionless.

He put the book on the soap-rack, picked up the yoghurt, made little finicky movements with the spoon. One of Matthias's rubber ducks was floating in the water beside him.

"I think it's about time you got out, then. That water's cold, Jo."

His white skin was very cold, and rough with goose-pimples.

Corrie began to speak with the dead-pan elocution of a lesson in a foreign language, pointing as he spoke.

"The water. The Johann. The chest. The asthma."

"The cough. The guts. The floor," Jo said. "I'll be all right."

He was very sensible about his asthma usually, and knew when to ask for his tablets, and when to go to bed.

Jo looked at him. "Any more news about that school?"

"No. Nothing new."

"What do you think will happen?" He looked intently at Corrie.

"The troops will go in, like they did with that plane. There's nothing else that can happen, is there?"

"They said they'll kill those children."

"No one was hurt in the plane."

The terrorists had made no concessions at all. They had severely injured a teacher and a child when they first attacked the school, and had refused to allow any medical assistance. The two bled to death, and their bodies had been thrown from the windows. They were still there, at the front of the building—no one allowed to approach near enough to remove them—together with the body of the first person who had died, a teacher who was helping children out of a first-floor window when the attack had started. Her body lay on the snow-covered grass, where she had fallen from the window when she was shot, a middle-aged woman in a neat grey suit, her spectacles lying on the path to one side of her. They had stared at the picture on the television when the news of the attack on the school was first broken, like people in a passing car looking at an accident in which they were not involved.

There were five terrorists in the school, three men and two women. They wanted eleven members of the Movement Eighteenth October freed from prisons in West Germany, each to be given DM120,000 and flown to a country of his or her choice.

Corrie could feel the edge of the bath through his jeans.

"That water *is* cold, Jo."

He stood up and held out his hands. Jo gave him the empty yoghurt carton and the book.

"Thank you, my good man."

"Out of the bath, Grandad, before you shrink away completely. There's not much left now."

"What time is it, infant?"

Jo's wrist was bare.

Corrie looked at his watch.

"The big hand's on nine, and the little hand's nearly on ten. Lilli's offering supper."

Jo stood up and pulled the plug out. He crossed his arms over his chest, shivering.

"O.K.?"

Jo nodded.

"I want to see the news on T.V."

The chain Jo was wearing round his neck had been sent to him by one of his old ladies. Over three years ago, when Mum had been heavily pregnant with Matthias, they had all appeared on television in a national family quiz programme. They lasted for several weeks, and got as far as the quarter-finals, losing on the last question, when Dad said that "All the world's a stage" was a speech from *Twelfth Night*. (He had wailed immediately he had said it, but the answer stood.) They all ostracised him for a week until he begged for mercy, and came down to breakfast one morning dressed in a sack, with some burnt twigs balanced on his head because he couldn't find any ashes. Jo had received fan mail from half the old ladies in England after these appearances, and answered them all. He still received Christmas and birthday cards from them.

"What's wrong, Jo?"

Jo began to take his jeans off.

"Nothing."

He could feel Jo's pain inside himself. He remembered when he had been very small—it might even have been before Jo was born—when he was covered with stings after blundering into a wasps' nest on the common. He could remember being beside himself with pain and panic, a pain too large and overwhelming for his body to be able to cope with, so that he curled up on the floor, whimpering, "Make it go away, make it go away," over and over again, hands half-raised as if to push the world away, his body rolling from side to side, and Mum had been there to make the pain go away.

"I'm the one who's known to be moody, aren't I?"

" 'He never says a word,' " Jo quoted. He had overheard two girls discussing Corrie in the High Street.

Corrie had never seen anyone with such thin legs as his brother. Dad called him Knitting-Needle Legs. Jo kept beating him up, but he wouldn't stop it. Jo, seeing Corrie looking at him, struck a few he-man poses, flexing his biceps, his face quite expressionless.

"Are you thinking about those terrorists?"

"No. Well, not really."

"Are you thinking about Mum again?"

Jo arranged his jeans very carefully on the rail that overhung the bath, aligning the edges precisely, his back to his brother. He concentrated on adjusting the jeans exactly as he wanted them. It was a while before he answered.

"A bit," he said eventually, his voice indistinct.

They were Levi jeans. Corrie looked at them, rather than Jo's thin bent back. He felt envious of Cato, who would always have little orange tags bearing his name sewn into the seams of the clothes he wore.

"Corrie?"

He couldn't see Jo's face properly, bent over in the dim light in the corner.

"Mmm?"

"Do you think that Matty remembers Mum? Do you think he still misses her?"

Corrie sat back on the lid of the lavatory pedestal.

"He cried a lot when she first left for Rome. . . . He cried a lot at first." Corrie paused, trying to sort his ideas out clearly. "I think, to Matty, she just went away on a journey one day, and didn't come back."

"But she promised him she'd come back. Does he think she's a liar? Does he think she's just left him? Remember how he kept asking when she was coming back?"

Jo turned.

"Do you still miss Mum?" he asked, looking directly at Corrie.

"Yes, of course I do."

"I thought it was just me."

Jo had been the one who had cried. Corrie remembered sitting beside him, with his arm around his shoulders for comfort, very pale in a new suit that was too big.

Jo pulled the towel around his shoulders, and they walked through into Jo's bedroom.

The record had come to an end, and Jo switched the record-player off. He awkwardly hitched at the towel, trying to stop it from falling off, as he slid the record back into its cover and then placed it in the box.

"When Mum had that operation, she would have known if it was very serious, wouldn't she?" He concentrated hard on his speech when he spoke seriously, like someone learning to read, straining over a few short words in a small child's picture-book.

"It was serious," Corrie answered, and then told Jo something he had never told him before. "The day before she went into hospital, I heard her crying in the bedroom. I'd come home early. She'd closed the door, but I heard her."

"Did you go in to her?"

"No. I didn't know what to do."

He had been twelve, Jo eight.

"She talked to me, the morning before she went." Jo was sitting on his bed, beside Corrie, drying between his toes. "She was listening to the *Saint Matthew Passion* when I came in. I was upset because she was going, and she said to me"—he concentrated carefully—"'If you want me to be there with you, play this music, and I will be there. If you want to think of me, think of me when you hear this music.'" He smiled as he looked up at Corrie. "That's how the records got so scratched. I used to put one of them on, and sit here with my eyes closed when no one else was there."

"She told me to look after you when she wasn't there."

Jo stood up and walked across to the map of Rousseau.

"In the dark and pathless forest."

"In the cold, sharp, shifting scree."

"In the moonless, starless silence."

"The Journey to the Inmost Sea."

"Tell me about Rousseau, Corrie."

"Rousseau is an island, and only we, amongst the non-Rousseaunians, know about it. Far away from the rest of the world, inaccessible, and impossible to find . . ."

Jo dressed slowly, listening as Corrie spoke, changing into fresh clothes. His T-shirt was an old and faded one, with a large smiling face on the front, like the one he drew inside the letter "o" of his name: the two dots, and the curve for the smile.

When he was dressed, and Corrie had finished speaking, Jo sat down again on the bed beside his brother, leaning in against him.

"Comfort me, boy."

Corrie put his arm round Jo's shoulders.

"Remember when I was younger, and you used to come in and sit on my bed when I was scared of the dark? You're my big brother!"

"Little though I am."

When he was younger, Jo had been frightened of going to sleep. He didn't understand where he went when he was asleep. He had told Corrie nothing about the nightmares he had been having lately, apart from saying that they were about darkness.

"How canst thou part sadness and melancholy, my tender juvenile?"

"Why tender juvenile? Why tender juvenile?"

"I spoke it, tender juvenile, as a congruent epitheton appertaining to thy young days, which we may nominate tender."

Jo grimaced. "We went a bit wrong there."

"A most acute juvenile!"

"Well, it was a long time ago."

"Back in the days when I was quite young, really."

It was two years since Jo had played Moth in *Love's Labour's Lost*.

"My first major triumph on the histrionic boards." Jo sighed with theatrical nostalgia.

"Your nine-year-old kneecaps caused quite a stir in those tights. Girls came from miles around just to ogle. When you turned sideways, whole rows fell over backwards."

"Like Guy Richens's grandmother."

"Showing her knickers."

Jo suddenly began to giggle helplessly, very high-pitched, like a very small boy, like Matthias. Tears ran down, splashed on to Corrie's shirt.

"Frankenstein and Mirth!"

He reached under his bed, and held up a parcel.

"Your present," he said, "cunningly removed from inside the wardrobe. Nearly time to open it. Let's go to supper, big brother. How do you feel on this, your special day?"

"Older."

"Well, you are pretty ancient now."

"Could you help me down the steps, young man?"

Jo gave Corrie his arm, and he began to stagger slowly towards the stairs, walking like someone very old.

11

LILLI didn't have a television, and she came through into their living-room when Jo switched on for the ten o'clock news.

It wasn't until the newscaster briefly added further details to earlier news stories of the day—the search for the murderers of the Turin kidnap victim, the latest casualty figures in the Paris bomb explosion—that they realised what was going to happen. The frightened child's face appeared again at the back of the newscaster, and the words "School Siege: Day Eleven," and then, abruptly, the picture on the television screen was the front of the West Berlin school, the three-storey bulk across the snow-covered field, from which the children's voices had come on Christmas Eve, singing "Der Tannenbaum."

The news programme was being transmitted live from West Berlin.

A reporter wearing a heavy coat stood in front of the camera, holding a microphone. There was noise all around him, a siren somewhere, a crowd in the distance, and floodlights illuminated the whole area in front of the school. The reporter kept glancing around him as he spoke.

There was one thing different about the front of the actual school building.

The last time they had seen it, every window had been dark, the whole of the school looking empty and uninhabited, but now one window in the middle of the second storey was brightly illuminated. The zoom lens of the camera moved in rapidly. In the centre of the window, sitting on an upright school chair raised so that she was fully visible above the sill, a little dark-haired girl, her hair in plaits, faced out across the newly fallen snow on the empty field.

It was ten minutes past ten. Almost half an hour ago the lights had been switched on to show the girl sitting there. She was the first child who was going to be shot by the terrorists. Just at the edge of the window, on the girl's right, was the figure of a woman with a gun. She had been described as a "girl of 28" in some of the newspapers, but she looked like a woman to Corrie. Her most recent act, before the attack on the school, had been the shooting of a West German politician's elderly invalid mother in her bed.

As the time moved nearer to quarter past the hour, the reporter gradually stopped talking and the sounds around him stilled. The area in front of the school suddenly became absolutely silent.

Corrie realised what was happening.

They were waiting for the sound of the gun.

There was a sound, sharp in the silence—the window in the illuminated room being opened outwards.

The little girl's face, in grainy close-up, was in the centre of the television screen, blurring in and out of focus as the cameraman tried to get the sharpest possible image.

"No," Jo said, beginning to get up. "They're going to show it happening."

Suddenly the camera jerked upwards, and all the lights in the area went out, inside and outside the school. There were screams from the unseen crowd behind the camera, a high-pitched shriek of metal as the microphone hit against something, and then a brilliantly bright explosion on the roof of the school and the sound of gun-fire from inside the building. Total confusion, glass smashing, voices shouting out harshly in the darkness, lit by the lurid flare.

As the camera righted itself, flames were gushing out from a window on the top floor of the school. The reporter poured out a flood of excited words. Figures ran in front of the camera, in the flickering light from the fire. Something fell from a window.

There was a lull in the noise and movement; then the doors at the front of the school were flung open, and children came running out across the snow.

In the ensuing confusion was the sound of a child's name being called over and over again, but the siege was over.

Towards the end of the news, the reporter said that it was believed that three terrorists, four children, and two soldiers were dead. One of the terrorists had been blown up by his own hand-grenade.

"Good," Jo said, with great viciousness. "Serves the bugger right."

Corrie and Lilli looked at each other, and then at Jo. He covered his face with his hands and turned to press himself in against the back of the chesterfield, drawing his knees up towards his chest.

L I L L I ' S was the last present Corrie opened. He opened it very carefully, trying not to tear the paper. She always wrapped her gifts beautifully.

They had carried supper through into the dining-room, clearing the game of Dungeons and Dragons from the table. The remains of Corrie's birthday cake were still in the centre of the table, and the fir-tree in the corner of the room.

They were sitting in the same places as on Christmas Eve, with Lilli opposite him, Jo beside him. Just before he lifted the final sheet of paper away, he looked up at her. He thought he knew what the present was going to be. She was watching him very intently, almost nervously.

" 'You look very thoughtful,' " Jo quoted, looking at her closely.

"I've been keeping something secret from you all," she said.

Corrie looked around for a gap amongst the paintings on the wall, but he couldn't see one. When the final sheet of paper was pulled away, he stared at the glazed painting for a long time in silence, his emotions confused, struggling to contain the wide smile of someone modest who has suddenly been extravagantly praised in public.

It was a new painting by Lilli.

Jo bent over beside him, and they studied the watercolour together, the size of a double-page spread in a book.

It was a painting of Corrie doing his homework at the kitchen table during the power cuts in January. In the soft glow of the candles he was facing straight out of the picture, his face rapt, as if committing the words of a play or a poem to memory, books and papers scattered on the table in front of him. The dresser was behind him, and every detail of the room around him was minutely recorded: the wooden weather-house, the Blue Denmark crockery, *The Wind in the Willows* calendar, the chiming pendulum clock, the enamel advertising sign for St. Bruno tobacco, the flowers in the Victorian jug, the Droste's cocoa tins, the Pears' soap advertisement, the pine plate-rack, the blue-and-white pottery village made by Mum on the top shelf of the dresser. The detail was so fine that he recognised the individual designs on the miniature Kate Greenaway playing-cards on the fridge door. The illustration on the queen of hearts card was for *I had a little husband*. A little girl stood at a table beside an open win-

dow. On the table were two jugs, and a tiny figure of a
man dressed in the scarlet tunic of a soldier. Corrie's eyes
returned to the figure of himself, at one side of the painting with its intensely realised interior, looking out at anyone looking at the picture. It was like looking into a
miniature mirror, into his own face.

"Corrie doing homework" was pencilled at the bottom,
and the signature was "Lilli Danielsohn," the name of a
woman from forty years ago. For a moment he felt that he
was looking back into the past, into the face of a boy from
long ago who was himself. He saw the face of the second
sister in "Fitcher's Bird," the face of a girl of about his
age, absorbed and inward-looking, although she was gazing out of the picture: the face of a girl intent on making
lace, reading a letter, playing a piece of music. Lilli's
draughtsmanship was as pure as when she was producing
her early work in the 1920s, the colours as delicate, the
details as finely observed.

"It's me" was all he could say, quietly.

Lilli looked around at the paintings on the walls.

"It's so long since I painted," she said. "I was frightened I wouldn't be able to do it. I wanted to produce
paintings like the work I did in Germany all those years
ago."

"It's just the same," Corrie said. "I feel as if I've been
given a famous painting from a museum. I feel like someone special."

"You are someone special. You're my grandson."

"Paintings?" Jo said, smiling. "You said paintings."

Lilli looked at them both, her blue eyes very intense.

"I have painted other pictures. I'm painting still. I feel
as though it's all starting to come back to me."

"When?" Jo asked, interested and excited. "You
haven't said a word about it to anyone. Have you?"

Lilli shook her head.

"No. This is the first one I've shown to anyone. I've been keeping secrets."

She stood up. "Come with me."

She moved to the door, beckoning them towards her.

"Magical revelations?" Jo asked.

Lilli smiled. "These are my hoards of precious stones."

They went into the hall, and through into the living-room at the back of the house. She made them go into the room in front of her, before she switched on the light, and then remained near the door as they moved inside.

The room was still uncarpeted, and the furniture covered with dust-sheets, but Lilli's easel stood in the centre, with a paint-covered smock hanging from it, and all round the wall at eye-level, unglazed, the heavy paper pinned directly against the wall, were at least twenty water-colours—the room seemed full of them—so rich and intricate that they seemed to nourish the sense of sight, and they were all of their family, and their home.

Lilli and Matthias side by side at the loom, bent over together absorbed, looking at the pattern as it began to emerge. The back of Tennyson's from the edge of the low cliff, seen through the burial-ground. The family on the lawn in summer sunshine, reading and talking around a picnic meal. The whole of the length of the sun lounge on a cloudy afternoon, with the connecting door open, Matthias painting at the table in the far part and Baskerville lying asleep in his basket amongst the scattered toys. Mum at the piano in Lilli's house, paintings on the wall behind her, Corrie's cello leaning against a chair. He, Jo, and Matthias at the edge of the sea, on the beach just beyond the end of the garden, Matthias holding his hand and about to throw a twig into the water for Baskerville. Mum and Matthias intent on a picture-book in Matthias's bedroom, beside the open window. Mum and Judith holding a sheet between them in the garden, beginning to fold it inwards towards each other, as Matthias, through the open window of the kitchen, knelt at a chair up against the sink, washing yoghurt cartons for Lilli's seedlings. Mum, Dad, Jo, and Matthias sitting around the breakfast table on a Sunday morning as Corrie adjusted the weights of the pendulum clock, as he did every Sunday morning. The Ferry House from across the playing-fields in autumn, with himself just visible practising his cello in the upper window, and Jo walking away with Baskerville at the end of a lead. Mum and Dad listening to music, tired, at the end of the day, in the living-room, books put to one side, the curtains drawn back from the window, the evening sky across the Green. The transient moments of a family in its home, engrossed in the everyday tasks of living and being together, were recorded and given permanence in the paintings which filled the walls, small-scale, intense, and deeply felt.

"This will be your birthday present," Lilli said to Jo, coming up behind them, and they looked at a painting of Jo asleep in bed, bedclothes twisted around him, books scattered on the floor, photographs, maps, and posters on the walls.

They were the first words anyone had spoken since they first came into the room. Corrie and Jo had moved slowly and attentively from painting to painting, not looking at each other.

Jo stopped in front of the painting of Mum at the piano, and caught at Corrie's hand as he moved past, as he had done when he was little and wanted to be taken on a walk. He spoke quietly, almost a whisper to himself.

" 'A Young Woman . . .' " He looked at Corrie.

". . .Seated at a Virginal.' "

They smiled at each other. A secret they shared with Dad.

"Mum."

They stood, finally, in front of the painting that was still on the easel.

It was a painting of the Victorian Evening, the moment just before Mum and Jo had started to sing "Won't You Buy My Pretty Flowers?" Dad was just glancing across from the piano at Corrie as he prepared to play the first notes on the cello. In the light from the oil-lamp, in front of the scrap-screen, Mum and Jo held their sheets of music and looked straight ahead towards the spectator, their faces very serious, drawing in their breath before the opening words.

"This is for your father," Lilli said. "It is the scene I tried to paint first, but I have only now completed it."

They gazed deeply into a scene that already lay within their minds, like memory given form.

"When did you paint them all?"

Jo's eyes had not left the painting as he asked the question.

"I made my first attempt on the day of your mother's funeral, Jo," Lilli said, quiet, matter-of-fact. "They were not paintings, just pencilled sketches. I wanted to draw some of the scenes I remembered with Margaret when they were vivid in my mind. I did not wish to mourn. I wished to remember the happiness in her life. I had wanted to draw for months before that, when I was still affected by the stroke, and, of course, I could not write down the pictures that were in my head. My hands worked against me."

She turned towards Corrie.

"The very first picture I completed—I had abandoned many others—was the one of you, Corrie, doing your homework. When I saw you in January, in the candle-light, the scene stayed in my mind. It brought back memories to me that I realised no longer gave me pain, and it was a scene, even then, at that time, I wanted to record. I painted that picture in May. Then all the other pictures came."

They walked back through into the dining-room, and sat around the fire, as they had done on Christmas Eve, before they opened the presents. Imperceptibly, they had drifted into the mood of their weekly teas together, when they first started to talk seriously to each other.

"I wanted to see whether I still had the skill. I destroyed so much of what I did at first, but I was determined. It made me fight the effects of the stroke more than anything else. Nothing would stop me. At the beginning of the year, you used to describe scenes for me to draw in your lessons, Corrie, as I began to improve. You were helping me to begin again, although you didn't realise. This Easter, I knew I would paint again, though I had told myself when I left Germany that I never would, ever again. In February I had a letter from an art gallery in West Berlin asking whether I would be able to help the director there, who was hoping to hold an exhibition of my work. They had collected first editions of all my books, and had tracked down some proofs that still existed, and had an almost complete survey of all my work. They asked if I would be willing to loan them any letters, or documents, or original paintings. I wrote back to him, and said that I had all my paintings, and that I would be happy for them to be on show again, for the people to look at them in the city where they were painted. I laid down some conditions of the way the exhibition had to be arranged."

They looked at the paintings on the walls around them.
She turned to them both, one after the other.

"I hope you will loan me your paintings—the English ones and the German ones—for the exhibition. They belong to you now, but I would like all the paintings to be together this one time in Berlin."

She indicated Corrie's birthday present on the table.

"The exhibition is to be next year, and the arrangements have now nearly all been made, but when the letter
came in February I thought, Could I paint anything now,
to add to my German paintings, to show that I am not like
someone who died forty years ago? Could I show that Lilli
Danielsohn is still alive, still capable of painting? So, in
the way I told you, I began to paint. In the sun lounge, in
the morning light, when you were all out, or at school, I
began. I hid everything like a thief. At first I was afraid I
would produce nothing I would like to show people, but
when I painted the picture of you in the candle-light, Corrie, I was happy. That was the scene I had inside my head
that I wanted to show other people. And so I painted
more. Then there were the designs and posters for *The
Winter's Tale*. I had become a painter again, and I wished
to show my family to other people who had never known
them, as I had done before."

She stood up, opened the door of a cupboard against
the wall, near the fir-tree, and took out a large framed
photograph. She held up the photograph and examined it
closely as she spoke.

"This photograph must be at the centre of the exhibition
in Berlin. It contains the source of all my paintings."

She began to talk to them, quietly and simply, of all
that she and Grandpa Michael had kept between themselves, the events that had destroyed her world.

She had come from a wealthy and cultured Dresden
family. Her grandfather Jakob Mitscherlich had owned the
biggest toy shop in the city, in Prager Strasse, the main
shopping street. Her father, a university professor spe-
cialising in German Literature, had been wounded, and
decorated, in the First World War, and her mother had
been a fashionable children's doctor. It was a large and
loving household—she had two sisters and three brothers

—surrounded by children, nieces and nephews, cousins, aunts and uncles, grandparents. In the early 1920s, a young woman, she had gone to Berlin, and achieved her great successes with her paintings, until the rise of the Nazis had made her and her family *Untermenschen*, sub-humans, and therefore disgusting. All the apparatus had swung into action against the millions of people who had no right to be treated as human beings, intensifying as the years went by. Those friends who were able began to leave the country, but her parents had decided to stay. Germany was their home. Most of her family, those who wished to leave, were trapped, unable to abandon children, or possessions, or sick or elderly relatives, or unable to get them out of the country. Her family persuaded her that she ought to leave when the opportunity arose after the events of *Kristallnacht*, when synagogues and houses burned, and the broken glass from Jewish homes and shops littered the streets throughout Germany. She had gone to England to work as a domestic servant—she knew no one in England, and her work had not been published there. She carried her paintings and sketch-books, and her parents' wedding-rings hidden inside a wooden toy, a little doll's cradle, that had been in her grandfather's shop before it was taken away from him. Germany was famous for its beautiful children's toys. She never saw any of her family again. They were lost in the immense, crowded darkness.

When she finished talking, quietly, without bitterness, she handed the photograph to them.

"This is my family," she said, "the family I had forty years ago."

There was no one he could recognise in the photograph as being Lilli, so she must have held the camera. They were all looking towards her.

Lilli began to identify who the people were.

The room in which they sat was the same as the one in

the painting of the christening scene in "Godfather Death." The same pattern to the plate, the same candlesticks, the same design on the silver, every painstaking detail of the painting. The scene was a long polished table illuminated by candle-light, just before a meal. The family —Lilli's parents and grandparents, her sisters and brothers, their sons and daughters, aunts, uncles, cousins, from the very elderly to a small baby—sat around the beautifully laid and decorated table, formal, consciously posed, everyone very still and serious, gazing into the camera. It was like a small ceremony for a leave-taking or a scene of private mourning, its emotions gentle and low-key.

The second sister from the painting for "Fitcher's Bird" sat half-way down the right-hand side of the table in a simple white dress, her arm around a boy of about five standing beside her, very upright in a dark suit, with a small girl, fair-haired, sitting on her knee. It was Lilli's youngest sister, Edda, and her two children, Florian and Dorothea, the Hansel and Gretel from the painting in his bedroom.

Lilli's sister was several years older in the photograph than in the painting, but completely recognisable. All around the table were the faces from the paintings: the Goose Girl, Rapunzel, the Girl Without Hands, the Fisherman and His Wife, Cinderella, the brother and sister from "The Juniper Tree," the Poor Boy in the Grave, Snow White.

Lilli's family peopled her paintings; their houses, rooms, and gardens were the settings. All around the dining-room were Lilli's memories of her family. There were twenty-seven people in the photograph.

He looked at the interiors of the pictures around him, and thought of those in the empty room next door, rooms in which families sat quietly together, the doors closed against the outside world, a world which would force open those doors and destroy all that it found inside after it had taken what it wanted, the silly family jokes of ordinary people, the school-books lying on the table, the unfinished knitting beside the chair, the photographs and pictures on the walls, the letters hidden away in drawers—all the noise and fury of the world reduced to the grief of individuals, families reaching out their arms trying to hold on to each other: Peter and Aline Goetzel and their daughter Lotte with her school photograph under glass and her notepaper with the elaborate letter "C" for Charlotte; the parents of Hanno and Hedwig Grünbaum, Ruth and Bernhard; Rudolf Seidemann's family; Ernst and Madeleine Jacoby, who had hoped their plan of emigrating to America would work, and their three children, Eugenie, Julius, and Lisette; Walter Werth's mother, Clara, and his twin sisters, Emmy and Doro, who sent him drawings of scenes from home so he wouldn't be homesick; Stefanie Peters's parents, and her little brother, who had just learned how to walk; Leonie Matthias; Nickolaus Mittler, his big brother, and his parents; Kurt and Thomas Viehmann's parents, Katherina and Wilhelm, and the rest of their family; the scores of others, all the family of his grandmother, all the people in all those pictures, the tiny few of the hundreds and thousands of families, all those millions of people, every one a person with memories and individuality, in every one of whom the world existed, like all the people in the book that Jo had been reading in the bath, the visitor's book from the living-room at Tennyson's that Mum had started years ago, with the dark green cover and *Unsere Gäste* embossed on it in gold.

Aidan, Eleanor, Lincoln, and Michael came to stay. House in chaos, but cuisine of usual high standard. Jo not quite walking yet.

Lovely gossipy evening. Music, singing, and talk. Michael and Lilli.

Safety note: don't sneeze in the sun lounge. Michael.

Champagne to celebrate Pieter and Margaret's four-teenth wedding-anniversary. Questionable vintage, but a very jolly body, but enough of Margaret. The champagne was splendid, too. Margaret, I love you! For God's sake push Pieter under a bus! Chris.

They've papered the walls at last. Max.

Now we are five. Welcome to our house, Matthias, from Pieter, Margaret, Corrie, and Jo.

Dropped in for coffee—stayed for tea! Sal.

Lilli's with us now.

Cadged another tea. Sal.

An evening of Bach from the Musical Meeuwissens. Margaret's pregnant AGAIN! Look out the London Phil-harmonic! Sal and Lilli.

Jo spoke first.

"Did Sal tell you that story about those hostages in Greece during the war?" he asked.

Corrie shook his head.

"A few years ago, she and Chris were on holiday in Greece. In the northern part. Before the divorce."

He looked up from under his neatly combed fringe at Corrie and Lilli, seeing that he had their attention. His eyes didn't leave theirs as he spoke, moving from one to the other, like a small child trying to gauge the feelings and moods of adults by the expressions on their faces, trying to see how he ought to behave.

"It was somewhere very remote, and a lot of guerrillas were there during the war. Because the Germans hadn't occupied it. One day the guerrillas made an attack. They had done it before, but this time they killed a lot of German soldiers. An ammunition dump or something. The local German commander was so angry that he . . ."

He paused, thought hard, then altered his sentence slightly, as though speaking the words of a fairy-tale to a child, where the words must always be the same, time after time, as the story is told at bedtime.

"The German commander was furious, and took all his troops to the nearest village. He made all the villagers gather together, and told them what had happened. He said that there was going to be a reprisal. He was sorry. But it was wartime. One male member of each household was going to be executed on the following morning."

Jo cast around for the right words to follow, chewing at his bottom lip, concentrating fiercely.

"The next part is the strange part. He told everyone to go home. They were to decide amongst themselves who was going to be the one to die in their household. Each family had to decide for itself."

There was a pause when he had finished speaking.

"What happened?" Corrie asked, at last.

"The following morning, the chosen hostages were all killed. Just as he had said."

Corrie thought about the quiet talking into the early hours of the morning, deciding who was to be chosen to die. Who had they chosen? Newly born babies who had only been alive for a few days; weak old men, towards the end of their lives? He imagined them, walking, or being carried, towards their deaths, followed by their grieving families.

Whoever had a child, whoever had a mother or a father, whoever had a friend, whoever was capable of feeling love, of forming a tie, of wishing to protect or care for another person, had a weakness that could be exploited, had a hostage in his life, someone he would give all he had in the world to protect from harm.

"On Christmas Eve," Jo said, "when you were reading 'The Wolf and the Seven Little Kids' to Matty, Corrie and I were sitting on the stairs listening."

Jo looked at Lilli, his face stern.

"The bit I always remember best in that story is the bit when the wolf goes to the miller and tells him to throw flour over his paws to disguise them." He began to quote from the story: " 'The miller thought to himself, "The wolf is going to harm someone," and refused to do as he was told. Then the wolf said, "If you do not do as I tell you, I will kill you." The miller was afraid, and did as he was told, and threw the flour over the wolf's paws until they were white. This is what mankind is like.' "

He repeated the final sentence.

" 'This is what mankind is like.' "

Lilli thought about what Jo had said. As she spoke, her German accent, as sometimes happened when she had a lot to say, became more and more pronounced.

"I suppose I should say something wise, something forgiving and fine to teach you all the goodness in mankind, but I have never been one of those people who believe that those who have suffered experience wisdom as an inevitable result of their suffering, become wiser and richer people. 'Suffering' sounds a grand word, as if I were someone special, someone who deserved a special hearing when opinions are expressed, but it is the word which truly expresses the feelings I had. I could never submit humbly in the face of the 'inscrutable will' of a God who had a purpose for a chosen people, a purpose in which all things that happened played a part. I raged when I was eleven and my oldest brother's baby died of a simple childhood illness. I raged when I was sixteen and my old aunt went blind. Why should a baby die? Why should an old woman go blind?

"We were never a religious family. My mother and father were very modern in their outlook, freethinkers. We were like a Christian family who are Christian only in remembering a little special celebration at Easter or Christmas, but for whom the idea of Christianity plays no conscious part in everyday life. I think it might have helped if we had been religious: we would have known that we had something we felt we were ennobled by suffering for. I could, perhaps, have rejoiced at such a death, going to see the unknown face of my certain God. But the faces I wanted to see were not unknown faces: they were the faces I already knew the best in all the world. We felt like people who were persecuted for being Christians, when we knew nothing of what being a Christian meant, and all because a distant relation, of whom we knew nothing, lit a candle in a church once, a long time ago. We were Germans, ordinary people, and then they told us that we weren't Germans, we were Jews. It would be like being told that you were no longer regarded as being English because you were a Christian, as if the one cancelled out the other.

"I shall never forget the grief and anger of what I saw and heard in those years in Berlin before I left, and I can never forget what happened to all those I loved. It would be a betrayal to forget. All my love was with them, and I felt that my love died when they died. No one had the right to expect me to be wise and noble and understanding when they died, and died in such a way. I wanted to kill the whole world. If I had believed there could be a God who had allowed all that to happen to serve His purpose, a cleansing fire from which the world would emerge clean and ennobled as if by a flood, I would have hunted God down and destroyed Him. 'This is what mankind is like.' Yes, I thought all mankind was worthy of contempt for what had happened, and the cleansing flood has brought filth and fear into every person's life.

"It is a Jewish custom, I think—this is something I have read, not something I have done or experienced; Jewishness is not something I know a great deal about—to leave a pebble at the graveside when you have visited the grave of someone you have loved, someone you love still, to show that you have been there and remembered him."

Lilli thought for a moment.

"My family, I believe, died in Auschwitz, after being in Theresienstadt, some of them, and I know no graves where I could lay a pebble, but I think of the Polish memorial for the dead on the site of Treblinka. I have seen a photograph in a book: the little area where one million people were put to death. Flat fields surrounded by evergreen trees are there, and thousands of pebbles, stones, and rocks sweep through the fields in broad paths. Each pebble is not a person. Each pebble is a village, each stone a town, each rock a city, and their sizes show the numbers brought there to that place to be killed, from the villages, towns, and cities of Europe—all those men, women, and children, rich and poor, all those different languages converging on a tiny remote place in Poland. In the centre of the fields amidst the stones and pebbles is a rock like a mountain: the stone for the people brought there from Warsaw to be killed, one third of all the people in that city. I think of all those empty houses, all those deserted streets.

"I felt that the wolf was knocking at the door, and I had no stones to sew inside him. I wanted him to come through the door and destroy me also. I felt that I could never find any stones: there is only sand in a desert. But, in time, I did find pebbles to lay beside their graves, and tiny pebbles mount up until they outweigh any boulders you can find at the edge of a mountain. Instead of turning my heart to stone, the pebbles sank all my bitterness, and I remembered the good things with happiness."

She turned to Corrie.

"Look again at the photograph. Do you notice anything about it?"

He answered at once, without even glancing at the photograph.

"It's the same room as in 'Godfather Death.' "

"Yes, but there's more than that. Look at the plate in the centre, near the front. Look at the knives and forks. Think of your birthday cake."

He looked at the plate in the photograph, and then went back to the table, carrying the photograph with him, and sat down.

It was the same plate as the plate on which his birthday cake stood, the plate that had been used for the Hansel and Gretel gingerbread house on Christmas Eve. The knives and forks they had used on Christmas Eve were the knives and forks in the photograph, with the letter "D" engraved on them in elaborate script.

"As things got worse for my family in Germany, they arranged to hide some of their possessions with friends who lived in the same street, a Christian family. Each night the neighbours came over with their baby granddaughter in her pram, and smuggled things back into their house in the pram, and hid them in one of their cellars. At the end of the war, a letter reached me from Germany, the first letter I had seen with a German stamp since the last letter I received from my mother. It was from the daughter of the woman with the pram, telling me she had possessions which were mine, kept safely for me. She and her husband and daughter came over to England to stay with Michael and me, and brought them with her. She told me that her mother had died in a concentration camp. She had spoken out against what was happening. She, with other Christians, had tried to help, tried to resist what was going on around them. 'This is what mankind is like,' Jo. There was a pebble there. I have the plates and the silver, and some of my mother's jewellery, and I know of people who tried to stop what was happening in their street. They belonged to no organisation. They were just our neighbours saying that something was wrong and should not happen, and some of them died for believing this. God would spare a city for one righteous man, but there were many little candle flames in all that darkness."

She picked up a book lying on the table beside her chair. It was *Children's Voices*, the new English edition of *Kinderstimmen*.

"One of the poems in this book, the very first one I illustrated, is by a Jewish woman poet from Berlin. She taught deaf-and-dumb children. She was taken to Theresienstadt at about the same time as my family, and then to one of the camps, and killed. I don't know—no one knows —when exactly she was killed, or where. She was taken to the concentration camp because she refused to leave her father when he was taken away. He was eighty years old. Her love for her father overcame everything else. 'This is what mankind is like.' There was another pebble there."

She turned the pages in the book, until she was looking at the final poem.

"Will you sing 'Auf meines Kindes Tod' again for me, Jo, just as you did on Christmas Eve? The tune is so beautiful."

Jo looked at Corrie.

"My cello's in the Ferry House."

"I'll sing it unaccompanied, then."

He stood up, and sang, his voice very true and piercing, the words that Corrie had set to music for "Hansel and Gretel."

> *"Von fern die Uhren schlagen,*
> *Es ist schon tiefe Nacht . . ."*

"Do you know what the title of the poem means, Jo?" Lilli asked when he had finished.

"On the Death of My Child."

"Do you know the meaning, word by word, of what you sang?"

Jo shook his head.

"Corrie wanted me to learn the German version for you. I only had a German edition to learn all the words. He explained what the poem was about. We looked at the painting."

He indicated the painting of the empty cradle, the man and the woman sitting across from each other on either side of a fire.

"It is a poem I often thought about when I was first in England. I had put all my illustrations away. When I looked at the empty cradle in my painting, I thought of the little empty cradle I had brought with me out of Germany, the little children's toy."

She looked across at Corrie.

"Corrie knows exactly what the words mean. He has read the English translation. His music fits the mood so precisely, and he has been able to express the emotions of other people. Listen, Jo, these are the words for which Corrie wrote the music."

Holding *Children's Voices*, she read the translation, slowly and quietly, the words that went with the music Corrie had written for the song in "Hansel and Gretel," the song for Florian and Dorothea Weisser.

> *"The clock strikes far away,*
> *It is already deep in the night,*
> *The lamp burns dimly,*
> *Your cot is made.*

> *Only the winds still go on*
> *Keening round the house.*
> *We sit lonely inside*
> *And often listen out.*
>
> *It is as though you were*
> *Going to tap gently at the door,*
> *As if you had only lost your way*
> *And were coming back tired.*
>
> *We poor foolish people!*
> *It is* we *who are still wandering,*
> *Lost in the horror of darkness—*
> *You have long ago found your way home."*

She passed the book over to Jo.

"They are beautiful words, and you wrote beautiful music, Corrie, but now it is only the first three verses that remain true for me. I cannot agree that death is where a child belongs, that a child is best out of the world, that death is the most comforting home for a child. We *are* wandering, we *are* lost in darkness, perhaps, in England, in Germany, over much of the world, but it is the children who will lead us out of this darkness, who will put an end to our wandering. With each child's birth, they say, the world begins again, and it is you who must use your life in trying to find a way, trying to light that darkness. This is what I truly believe."

She turned towards Jo.

"Will you sing again for me, Jo—in English this time?"

Corrie was still sitting at the table.

As Jo sang, Corrie looked at the painting of himself in the candle-light, and at the candle-light of the photograph, all Lilli's family grouped around the table at the beginning of a meal. In "Godfather Death" the poor man had refused to allow God to hold his child as His godson at its christening because God left the poor to starve; rejected

the Devil because he led men into evil; and chose Death as
his child's godfather because Death made all men equal,
and made no distinction between rich and poor. When his
godson was grown up, Godfather Death led him deep into
the forest and gave him his present, the skills which would
make him a rich and famous physician: a secret herb to
cure ills, and the power of telling if a person was going to
live or going to die. Whenever the godson was with a
patient, Godfather Death would appear, and if he stood by
the patient's head, he would recover, but if he stood by the
patient's feet, that person belonged to Death and the godson was forbidden to use the herb to cure him. At the end
of the story, after the godson had defied Death to save the
life of a king's dying daughter, Death took the young man
deep below the surface of the earth into a cave where
countless candles burned, millions upon millions of them,
flickering, rising up, and dying away perpetually, the lights
of the lives of all the people in the world, and showed him
the candle of his own life, tiny and guttering, and when the
young man pleaded with him to light a new candle for
him, out of love, so that he could marry the king's daughter and live the rest of his life in happiness, Godfather
Death threw the little piece of candle down to the floor of
the cave, so that it was extinguished and the young man
belonged in the hands of Death for ever.

He remembered the candles of his birthday cake, and of
Christmas Eve, when the fir-tree was covered with candles
and the whole room swayed and swam with their flames.
That was how they had staged the final scene of *The
Winter's Tale*. Leontes, Perdita, Paulina, and Polixenes
moved silently towards the statue of Hermione in the
chapel, hardly visible in the dark centre of the stage, beneath the white wood of the dying tree, behind the banks
of unlit candles, and in a long sequence without any di-
alogue, as his music was played by the consort off-stage,

as Jo began to sing, they took tapers, knelt before the statue of the wife who had died of grief, and stood to light the candles, one by one; and Hermione became bright and visible in the warm, shifting glow. After sixteen years of winter, a barren mountain and perpetual storm, tears shed daily at the grave of a wife and child buried together, Leontes's wife returned to him from death, as music played, as the tree burst into blossom and fruit—a warm and living woman, candles lit to light all the candles that had gone out in their world.

ALMOST blinded with tears, Gretel stumbled towards the well, the water falling unheeded from her eyes. She tried to remember what her brother had said to her, to comfort her, when he was there beside her, and could speak to her, and give her courage. "God will not forsake us," he had said. "Don't believe that we can ever be totally abandoned."

"Dear God, please help us," she cried in her despair. "If the wild animals in the forest had torn us to pieces, at least we would have died together. I'm so frightened of being all by myself."

"Stop that noise!" the woman sneered. "It won't do any good at all. No one can hear you, and no one will come and help you. Your brother dies tomorrow."

Early the next morning, when it was still dark, the woman made Gretel get up, light the fire, and hang up the cauldron full of water. Outside the windows, the snow was still falling.

"We will bake first," the woman said. "I've already heated the oven, and the dough is all kneaded and ready."

She took Gretel over to the oven, from which the flames were already darting.

"Creep in," said the woman, "and see if it is properly heated for the bread."

Gretel thought of her brother's words, and then of her brother. She looked at the oven, and then at the woman, thinking rapidly.

"Into there?" she said. "Into the oven? How on earth can I do that?"

"You little fool!" said the woman. "Are you totally helpless? It's easy enough for anyone, even a child. There's plenty of room to get in through the door. Look, I'll show you."

She pushed Gretel to one side, and leaned forward into the oven.

"Like this," she said, her head entirely inside. "Like this," her voice echoing and hollow.

With all her strength, Gretel gave the woman a tremendous shove that knocked her right into the middle of the oven, and shut the iron door, and fastened the bolt.

The woman began to howl with pain and anger, but Gretel instantly ran out of the house, and the godless witch perished in the flames.

Gretel ran like the wind to the back of the house, through the deep drifts of snow to the little stable, to the iron cage where Hansel was imprisoned.

"Gretel?" Hansel called out when he heard someone approaching. "Is that you, little sister?"

Gretel flung open the door of the cage, crying, "Hansel, we are safe! The witch is dead!"

Then Hansel sprang out like a freed bird, and they flung their arms around each other, laughing and crying in their joy.

Hand in hand, they ran through the snow back into the house, and, in one of the rooms in the long corridor, found hoards of precious stones.

"These are a lot better than pebbles!" said Hansel, dropping them into the pockets of his coat until they were both crammed full, and Gretel filled her pinafore.

"We must go now," said Hansel. "We must leave this dark forest, and never come back."

He took his little sister by the hand, and they began to walk.

As they walked, the sun began to rise, and, in the warmth, the snow began to melt from the branches of the trees, sparkling water falling all around them as the green of the trees emerged.

After several hours of walking in warmth and light, the trees beginning to thin around them, grass now growing beneath their feet, they came to a great river, clear and calm in the green solitude. Beyond the trees, beyond the river, open green fields stretched emptily away towards a wide horizon.

"We cannot cross out of the forest," said Hansel. "I can't see a bridge, not even a plank."

"There's no ferry either," Gretel replied, "but there's a white duck swimming there. I'm sure she'll help us, if I ask her."

Then she stood on the river bank and sang.

> *"Little duck, little duck, the river's so wide*
> *Hansel and Gretel beg you for a ride.*
> *There's no way across for us, no bridge in sight,*
> *Please take us across on your back so white."*

The duck immediately swam across to them, and let Hansel sit himself on her back.

"Sit beside me, little sister," he said, making a place for her.

"No," Gretel replied. "That will be too heavy for the little duck. She shall take us across, one after the other."

The little duck did this, and they were soon safely across the river.

When they had walked for a short time, their surroundings seemed to be more and more familiar to them, until, in the distance, they saw their father's house.

Hand in hand, they began to run across the green fields.

As they drew nearer, they saw their father, very still, sitting in a chair beside the door, like a very old man, his head bowed.

"Father!" Hansel and Gretel shouted. "Father!"

Slowly, their father looked up.

He had known no moment of happiness since he had left his children in the forest, and had spent his life in mourning since that time.

He stood up, as they ran towards him, holding out his arms, tears running down his cheeks.

He threw his arms around them, embracing them as if he could never again bear to be parted from them.

"Oh my daughter, oh my son," he whispered, "forgive me for what I have done. You are my beloved children. Stay with me. Stay in your father's house."

They poured the precious stones at his feet. He didn't even look at them, but gazed into his children's eyes.

They are together still, happy and contented, living in perfect comfort and prosperity, a devoted family, away from the world, at the edge of the forest.

My story is ended now.

Acknowledgements

I AM GRATEFUL for permission to quote from the following texts:

The Diary of Anne Frank: Translated from the Dutch by B. M. Mooyaart-Doubleday. First published 1947 in Holland by Contact, Amsterdam. Copyright © 1958 by Vallentine, Mitchell & Co., Ltd.

"Children's Crusade," by Bertolt Brecht: English translation by Hans Keller copyright © 1969 by Stefan S. Brecht. Reprinted by kind permission of the Estate of Bertolt Brecht.

Emil and the Detectives, by Erich Kästner: Copyright 1929, 1931 by Doubleday & Company, Inc. Reprinted by permission of Doubleday & Company, Inc.

The House at Pooh Corner, by A. A. Milne: Published by Methuen & Co., Ltd.

The Wind in the Willows, by Kenneth Grahame: Copyright by the University Chest, Oxford.

A Calendar of German Customs, by Richard Thonger: Copyright © 1966 Oswald Wolf (Publishers) Ltd. Quoted on page 36. "On the Death of My Child": Translated from the German by Leonard Forster. From *The Penguin Book of German Verse*, page 313. Copyright © 1957, 1959 Leonard Foster. Reprinted by permission of Penguin Books, Ltd.

The Children's Haggadah: Edited by Dr. A. M. Silberman. Published in 1937 by Shapiro, Valentine & Co.

The versions of the stories by the Brothers Grimm are based upon the translations by Margaret Hunt and James Stern in *The Complete Grimm's Fairy Tales*. Copyright 1944 by Pantheon

Books, Inc. Copyright renewed 1972 by Random House, Inc. Published in Great Britain by Routledge and Kegan Paul in 1975.

I hope that the dedication at the beginning of this novel, which includes all the above authors, expresses my gratitude to them.

A Note About the Author

PETER RUSHFORTH was born in County
Durham, England. He was educated at the
universities of Hull and Nottingham. He presently
lives, and teaches, in a North Yorkshire village.
Kindergarten is his first novel.

A Note on the Type

THE TEXT of this book
was set on the Linotype in Garamond,
a modern rendering of the type first cut by
Claude Garamond (1510–1561).
Garamond was a pupil of Geoffroy
Tory and is believed to have based his
letters on the Venetian models,
although he introduced a number of
important differences, and it is to him
we owe the letter that we know as
old-style. He gave to his letters a
certain elegance and a feeling of
movement that won for their creator an
immediate reputation and the patronage
of King Francis I of France.

Composed by The Maryland Linotype
Composition Corporation,
Baltimore, Maryland
Printed and bound by
The Haddon Craftsmen, Inc.
Scranton, Pennsylvania
Book design by
Margaret McCutcheon Wagner